COSMIC
GROOVE

HAND OF FATE - BOOK FIVE

COSMIC GROOVE

HAND OF FATE - BOOK FIVE

SHARON JOSS

AJA PUBLISHING
USA

COSMIC GROOVE
Copyright © 2017 by Sharon Joss
All rights reserve.

Published 2017 by Aja Publishing
www.ajapublishing.wordpress.com

Book and cover design Copyright © 2017 by Aja Publishing
Cover art & design by Lou Harper
© iStock_000012776765_Illustration
Heraldic Griffin Design Copyright © by Buch / Dreamstime

Sign up for my new release mailing list at: http://bit.ly/1MhS3lb
Your email will never be shared and you can unsubscribe at any time.

QUALITY CONTROL: We care about producing error-free books. If you find a typo or formatting problem, send a note to sharonjoss.author@ gmail.com so that it may be corrected.

PRINTED IN THE UNITED STATES OF AMERICA

ISBN: 978-1-941544-43-3

Also by Sharon Joss

THE COLD AIR was a shock after the heat inside the car. I trudged determinedly through snow-carpeted apple orchards behind Knutt's Apple Farm. Snow and frozen leaves clung to my boots. Recent heavy weather had stripped the trees of their remaining leaves, and they waved their newly naked branches to a watery sky. In spite of two pair of wool socks, my toes were already turning all ice-cubey. I clenched my gloved hands into fists and kept going.

A passing cloud dimmed the weak sunlight even further. We'd likely see more snow tonight.

"Keep an eye out, Blix—no, wait." My sphinx-form djemon halted a dozen feet ahead of me, one clawed front talon curled daintily out of the snow. While djemons do not suffer from extremes in temperature like humans, Blix is a creature of the desert, and far prefers the dry warmth of his heated dog bed.

"What I mean is, um, *let me know* if the bad guys

9

show up, okay?"

I've learned to be careful with how I communicate with Blix. He doesn't yet understand slang. He would pluck one of his own eyes out in an instant, if I asked him to.

"Of course," he answered, and then scampered up the slope, as graceful as a young cat. Black and hairless, he's got a pair of splendidly feathered wings and a long prehensile tail with a tuft on the end makes him look much more elegant than it sounds. Large, bulbous yellow eyes and a gargoyle-like expression give him a mug only his master could love. In this case, that would be me.

It took me considerably more effort to join him at the crest of the hill overlooking the cemetery. I paused to catch my breath, releasing great gouts of steam into the frigid air. Physically, the bruising in my lungs had dissipated, but any sort of exertion burned like fire. The blue plastic brace I wore beneath my parka severely restricted movement. Right now, it felt more like a torture device than an appliance of healing. The only reason I was still wearing it was that it helped with the muscle spasms.

When the Nalusa Falaya tossed me against a tombstone on Halloween night, I'd been broken in more ways than one. Three weeks later, I was *almost* positive I didn't need the brace anymore. As Morta's Hand on Earth, I heal extraordinarily fast, but that doesn't mean it doesn't hurt like the dickens. The chest brace was meant to limit movement. It was a cruel master.

The immense yew tree at the bottom of the basin stood tall and dark against the pristine surroundings—a reminder of my failure.

Two people had died here.

Maybe a djenie as well. I choked back a sudden lump in my throat. *Oh Rhys.*

In daylight, the snow-covered vale looked almost peaceful. Someone had toppled the trio of stone altars where the witch-cult leader John Fewkes and his sister Liddy had murdered Lou Scali, my friend and mentor. They'd very nearly sacrificed Honey Briscoe and her son Arby as well, in a vile ritual to release an immortal demon. Once freed, the Nalusa Falaya granted John Fewkes immortality and great powers of black sorcery.

Now, two immortal evils had been loosed upon the world, and the death toll was climbing. I wasn't sure where John Fewkes was dining, but the Nalusa Falaya preferred human prey.

I stumbled down the faint trail, willing my leaden feet to move faster. For every step I took toward my goal, the air temperature seemed to drop a degree. It was darker here; the weak winter sun scarcely penetrated the thick boughs of evergreen.

I reached for the rough bark of the ancient yew with trembling hands. Nothing.

I leaned against the bole, pressing my cheek against the sapwood. He had to be there. "Rhys, it's me."

In my mind, I sensed...something. And then he was there. I felt his agony—recognizing as I did, that it was only a pale shadow of what he was experiencing. *Get me out of here!*

Pain and despair welled up within me, along with the certainty—*He's alive!*

For now.

Djenies are tough, but not immortal. The yew tree's poison would eventually kill him. Already, the incandescent blaze of Rhys' life force life was fading.

"I'm here, Rhys." I choked on the words. "I swear I'll get you out of there." I pressed closer to the tree's wide unforgiving trunk, so broad; my arms could not encircle the half of it. "I'll find a way, it whatever it takes. Don't give up on me!"

Tears streamed down my cheeks. I caressed the gnarled bark, yearning for Rhys, overwhelmed by the depth of his echoed misery. To a djenie, there was no torture greater than that of imprisonment. The old cliché of the genie in a bottle was a nightmare for Rhys and his kind. And now this alien trap, intended as a demon's prison, held Rhys. Great stars, I had to do something. I *had* to find a way.

I inspected the trunk, searching for a seam or crack in the rough bark, but the light was bad and getting worse. I sent Blix up into the branches. "You see anything?"

Blix scampered up and around the trunk like a monkey, disappearing into the dense foliage. He answered me with a forlorn squeak.

"Nope," I said, pulling my wool watchman's cap lower. The air was getting colder. "You have to say it. How do I open the tree?"

He bounced down to the lowest branch and licked his lips with a pointy blue tongue. "You think this is a tree, and it looks like a tree, but it is not a tree." He cocked his head. "It is better to think of this creature as an anemone or a clam. It can open and close at will. The bark camouflages the seams, which are a mere cell's width wide."

Blix had only recently begun to speak. His new voice had not yet settled into a timbre. Djemons are ageless beings, and do not go through the same language acquisition phases that humans do. His voice had a raspy, transgendered quality to it—sort of a cross between Tom Waites and Tina Turner.

"So, in other words, impossible." I stepped back and gave the immense trunk a half-hearted kick. I would never forget Rhys' stunned expression as he was impaled on a spar within the tree. His agonized scream as the trunk and limbs closed up around him still echoed in my head. How could I live with myself, knowing this was my fault?

"I am saying that brute force is not the answer you

seek," Blix said.

Without warning, he arched his back and hissed at me, his teeth bared.

"What's the matter?"

The hiss grew louder, filling the air around us.

My djemon gave a loud squeak of terror and disappeared.

Iridescent black smoke materialized around the base of the tree, choking me with the stench of blood and pine and despair. The smoke thickened and blackened—congealing some twenty feet above me. Swamp lights whirled like angry wasps within it. The sooty vapor stretched into a vaguely snake-like form— the Nalusa Falaya.

Too late, I realized how vulnerable the plastic brace around my chest and neck made me.

The mist moved like a cobra, extending its body, writhing across its own length until it lowered his head to mine, sniffing me, head to toe. It had me backed up against trunk—I had nowhere to go. Up close, it was more than just teeth and eyes. Floating somewhere beneath the veil of black smoke, was a nose, a chin, a suggestion cheekbones.

"Mmmmmm." It said. Closer it came, sniffing my hair, my shirt, and like a rude ghost-dog, at my crotch. "Mmmm."

I tore open the door in my mind to Morta; goddess of Fate and the ruler of the undead. As her power warmed me, the sound of distant war drums began to beat, echoing in my head—giving me a surge of confidence.

No mere demon can scare me.

"I am the Hand of Fate," I said. "Hear me and obey!"

In answer, the monster exhaled in my face, its double row of sharp teeth mere inches away. They looked a lot more solid than the rest of the creature. The awful, choking stench of rotting flesh rolled over me and I coughed.

A spasm of white-hot pain twisted along my spine. My ribs burned—I grunted against the agony and sucked a shallow gasp of air through my clenched teeth.

"I hereby banish the Nalusa Falaya from all physical and metaphysical earthly planes, never to return!"

Nothing happened.

I panted, gritting my teeth against the vise-like cramp in my back and tried again. "I banish the creature known as the Nalusa Falaya from any and all physical planes, never to return!"

The warmth of Morta's power began to fade, leaving only an icy chill.

Oh great. The one time I really needed it, and it wouldn't work against the Nalusa Falaya.

The monster demon nosed me again—harder, this time. "Muuuse," it whispered.

Another wave of demonic halitosis washed over me. *What the hell?* It could've eaten me already, if it wanted to. What did it want? "Get away from me," I said, flexing my left hand. My shears couldn't cut smoke, but they made me feel better.

"Muuuuuuuse," it insisted. It reared up like a viper, arching over me, and bellowed, "GIVE ME MUUUUUSE!"

I fell to the ground, flat on my back, feeling as vulnerable as Wyle E. Coyote beneath the descending shadow of an Acme safe. A roaring sound filled my ears. I felt as if I'd stuck my finger into an electric socket. My mouth tasted tinny.

I gasped, feeling another cough coming on. I rolled to my side, fighting it. "Blix," I groaned. "Help me!"

I panted, willing the cough away. What the hell was that about? *Does it think I'm a Muse? Does it want music?* I managed get to my knees.

A bark-like *Krak* answered. A flapping of wings sounded from my left, and the cloying stench of smoke was gone. The clenching spasm in my back began to ease.

"No, Blix. You have to say it."

A raven the size of a Labrador retriever swaggered into view. A chill of fear swept through me. It could only be the cultist sorcerer, John Fewkes.

Oh god no. I scuttled away from him, on hands and knees—cursing the brace that hampered my every movement. The Fewkes-raven thing flew at me, battering me about the shoulders with his wings, tearing my parka to shreds until he was scrabbling at the hard plastic of my brace with his clawed feet. He pecked at the back of my head—hard; trying for my eyes. His kraak-kraaking sounded like malevolent laughter.

I managed to scramble to my feet even as he buffeted me with his body and wings. My wool cap was gone. His heavy beak thunked against my skull like it was a ripe melon. Warm blood trickled behind my ears.

"Get him, Blix!" The Fewkes-raven thing hit me again and I went sprawling. The only shelter was the Penfield family burial vault—perched halfway up the vale, amid a copse of evergreens. If I could make it there, maybe I could keep him off me. I covered my head with my hands to protect my face. The raven went for my gloves, shredding the leather like it was tissue. Bloody droplets stained the snow. Between the weight of the thing and the fricking chest brace, I couldn't get up.

And then Blix barreled into him, knocking him loose. I clambered to my feet and tottered up the hill. Blix weighed less than ten pounds—he wouldn't be able to hold off Fewkes for long.

I made for the Roman-inspired colonnade of the tomb while they were till scrapping in the snow.

Behind the columns, the shallow portico and entrance welcomed me, offering everlasting sleep of the dead, but I wasn't buying. At least, not yet.

It was colder here under the evergreens surrounding the crypt, but at least there was no snow. I scanned the bare earth for stones and snatched up a few. The Fewkes-raven had my little djemon held firmly in its beak, and was clawing at him with its sharp claws, trying to gouge his eyes out.

I stepped away from the shelter, and let fly with a marble-sized pebble. The brace affected my velocity, but not my aim.

Fewkes took a solid hit in the eye. He squawked in pain and Blix squirmed free and winged toward me like a bat out of hell. I was about to fire off another, when a shadow passed overhead.

Damn, the Nalusa Falaya hadn't left.

I hustled back inside the vault, with Blix right beside me. There was no door—not that any barricade would stop the Nalusa Falaya--or John Fewkes, for that matter. A trickle of blood dripped into my eye, and I wiped it away. I ripped off the shreds of what once were my gloves. My hands were covered with blood. My blood.

While the Fewkes-raven perched out of range atop a toppled gravestone, the Nalusa Falaya circled the crypt, moaning. Wordlessly beseeching. Like it wanted something.

From me.

Weirdly, this was the second time the Nalusa Falaya could have killed me, but hadn't even tried. At the summoning, it had tossed me aside like a bad penny, instead of eating me, like it had Liddy Fewkes. It had hadn't been aggressive toward me in the least. Hitting that gravestone was just bad luck on my part. I huddled in the depths of the tomb, my heart pounding, my hands and feet numb with cold. Blix crouched in the doorway, lashing his tail in agitation, his head swiveling toward every sound. After a long while, he sneezed, and seemed to relax.

Cautiously, I ventured a peek outside. Both the raven and demon were gone.

Relieved, I checked Blix over; running my hands over his unnaturally warm body, looking for wounds I knew had already healed.

"Come on; let's get out of here before we freeze to death."

But as soon as I stepped away from the vault, the Fewkes-raven swooped down on me from the thick pines overhead. I ducked back inside, but not before catching a glimpse of the great black snake form of the Nalusa Falaya coiled up on the roof of the crypt. He looked pretty comfortable up there. And solid enough that he was no longer transparent.

I was hosed—caught like a rat in a trap.

I cursed my own stupidity, pacing back and forth

in the enclosed space, my hands tucked into the tattered pockets of my ruined parka. As I paced, my eyes gradually adjusted to the gloom inside the shrine. Nine clumsy steps in each direction—a marble-lined walk-in freezer. Even the floor was marble. Probably cold enough to make ice cubes in here year-round. A girl could freeze to death out here.

Yeah.

I'd left my cell phone in the car—the battery was dead. No one knew I was here. And who would I call, anyway? Henri was down in Florida for the winter. I hadn't heard from Lance in months. Lou Scali was the only person who might have known where to look— and he was dead. I couldn't send Blix for help, because, well, he's a demon. The only people I'd let know about Blix were wither djenies like Rhys and Henri, or other demon masters, like Charlie. Some secrets you take to the grave.

"They're playing with us," I said, as much to myself as to Blix. "If they really wanted us, they could just come in and drag us out."

Blix perched on the narrow ledge of the pediment above the entrance, flicking his tail in agitation. The tomb reminded me of the Roman temples I learned about in high school Latin class. It was old, I knew. Not Roman old, but at least a couple centuries. Maybe that's what people in the olden days thought heaven looked like—a Roman temple. There were even decorations on the inside. Carvings. I thought of all the tumbled tombstones outside in the cemetery and silently gave thanks to whoever had built this vault for his final resting place. Whoever built it, had built it to last.

"I await your command."

That was Blix' way of saying he didn't know what I wanted from him. It was a step up from licking his eyeballs, which creeped me out no end, but wasn't much help. We were still working on our communication skills, Blix and me.

A noise from behind me made me jump, but there was nothing there. An echo, maybe. I clapped my hands over my icy ears, cursing the loss of my cap. If I stayed in here much longer, frostbite was a real possibility.

I wondered if John Fewkes felt the cold in his raven form. I sure hoped so. Served him right. Not the Nalusa Falaya, though. It was not a creature of flesh and blood. Like Blix, it could probably sit up there all night waiting for me to come out.

But why? *It wants something.* Does it think I'm a muse? *Yeah, right.* Not likely. Or did it mean music? "Hey Blix, what kind of music do demons like?"

Blix shook out his wing feathers and frowned. "Music means nothing to me. Only your voice," he said. "I do not understand the appeal of any other sound. I existed for an eternity, awaiting my name day. On that day, I heard your voice for the first time, and it is the sound of your voice saying my name that I prefer above all other sounds. I believe this is true of most of my kind."

Blix had given me an excellent answer—but his response also played to my ego. Both Henri and Rhys had schooled me not to praise him for answering a question in this manner. If I praised him for feeding my ego, he would quickly evolve into a creature that existed only to flatter me. If I wanted a useful and helpful djemon, I had to be careful about how I expressed myself to him.

This is the thing about being a demon master that most people don't realize. Raising a demon is a huge responsibility.

On the other hand, I noticed that the Nalusa Falaya didn't seem to be paying any attention to John Fewkes, which kind of went against the whole master and demon protocol. Fewkes didn't even appear to be in control of his demon. "That's not what I meant, Blix. What do you think the Nalusa Falaya wants?"

"I believe it wants Muse."

"Duh, but what do you think Muse is?" I wiped my runny nose on my sleeve.

"A djemon is anchored to its master via the soul. If the Nalusa Falaya is a djemon, I would expect that Muse is its master."

"That can't be right. I banished John Fewkes'

djemon during the ritual, and it left a gaping hole in his soul. The Nalusa Falaya was pulled into that void. Fewkes and the Nalusa Falaya are bound together, no different than you and me."

"I think not," Blix answered. "I believe that the relationship between John Fewkes and the Nalusa Falaya is more like the bond between Charlie Crimmer and Annie. Annie once answered to another master. Perhaps the same is true with the Nalusa Falaya."

"True enough," I agreed. Annie had originally belonged to Miriam Woo. When Annie—who had been very small at the time—was torn loose from Mimsy's soul by Papa Shango, she very nearly perished. I'd accidently torn a hole in Charlie Crimmer's soul, and when I brought the two of them together, each had healed each other. I had anticipated that John Fewkes would die when I ripped his very large djemon from his soul, but instead, the Nalusa Falaya taken its place.

"What do you think it wants from me?"

Blix shrugged, as only a djemon can do. "You are Fate's Hand. Perhaps it believes you can give it Muse."

"How could it possibly think that? And why me? We haven't exactly been introduced." With nothing else to go on, I mulled over the riddle as I paced. It certainly did seem to believe I was connected to Muse—be it music or a person, or...whatever.

The tomb was getting colder by the minute. I don't know how long we'd been in there, but the light was fading. The entire vale was in shadow. I sent Blix out for a look-see. He was back in less than a minute, giving me the all-clear. Cautiously, I stepped outside; going just far enough to see that there was nothing on the roof. Time to go.

We set off for the car. Silently, I cursed the chest brace and my clumsiness with every step. I don't know if it was the cold or my imagination, but as we left the deep shade beneath the pines and headed up the hill, I could swear I heard the sobs of a weeping woman echo across the vale.

CHAPTER 2

DARKNESS COMES EARLY in winter—the gloom of dusk had deepened by the time Blix and I reached Knutt's empty lot where I'd parked the car. It took me three tries to get my keys out of my pocket, and they fell through my numb fingers to the pavement. Of course the stupid brace didn't make it easy for me to see them, and harder still to retrieve them. Gripping the car's door handle for support, I eased myself to the pavement, blindly searching for the keys. In spite of my care, I slipped on the icy asphalt and landed on my ass. A jolt of pain shot up my hip and my back seized up into another spasm.

I rolled to my side, squirming futilely to escape the pain. "Get the keys, Blix." I gasped. A moment later, my little djemon closed my stiff fingers around the icy keys and disappeared. All I could do was lie there, waiting for the spasms to subside.

The sound of a car turning into the parking lot caught my attention. A Monroe County Sheriff's car pulled up beside the Honda.

With the flashlight in my eyes, I couldn't see who it was, but whoever it was couldn't miss my shredded parka. I held up my hand against the light.

"Watcha doin' there, Mattie?" I knew his voice immediately.

I grinned in spite of myself. Sheriff Jim Reynolds likes me. "B-b-boy am I glad to see you." My teeth clattered from the cold. "Thought I was going to end up a p-popsicle."

He helped me to my feet, his sharp glance taking in the dried blood on my hands. "What the hell have you been up to," he asked, brushing the snow off me. "Where's your hat? You're hurt."

"No, I'm fine."

"There's blood in your hair."

"Oh, um. Yeah." I remembered, patting the matted, frozen strands. "Um, it's a long s-story." I couldn't stop my teeth from chattering.

He opened the back door of his patrol car. The heater was on full blast. "Get in."

I think I must've moaned—my legs were pretty unsteady. He helped me get in. "Th-thanks," I said. "All I need is a few minutes--." It was like heaven in there.

"Denny's okay?"

"Whatever." I wanted to curl up into a ball and go to sleep right there.

Thirty minutes later, we were seated at a four-top at Denny's in Webster. Reynolds had wrapped me in a wool blanket from the trunk of his car and given me his own wool watchman's cap. I'd made him help me get the danged chest brace off. It sat in a chair across from me in mute disapproval. I'd already polished off a plate waffles and sausage, smothered in hot maple syrup, and had my hands wrapped around giant cup of hot chocolate. The warmth in my belly was making good headway to thawing out the rest of me.

I told him I'd slipped and cracked my head on a gravestone. Of course Reynolds didn't believe me—he's too good a cop for that, but he let me slide, and for that I wanted to tell him what happened. But first, I wanted some time to think about it. It wasn't just that I'd failed to banish the Nalusa Falaya. There was something about that cemetery that had unsettled me. Something different. Something I couldn't quite put my finger on.

"What were you thinking, going out there alone?" Reynolds asked.

"I had to go. I had to see where it happened." I shook my head. My toes and the tips of my ears itched like crazy, but that was a good sign—I was thawing out. "I guess I still can't believe that Fewkes and the cult managed to summon a demon." In spite of a news helicopter flying over the ritual site, the riot in Mumford had gotten the lion's share of news coverage, and been blamed on mass hysteria following a power outage. I guess a coven meeting on Halloween night to summon a demon wasn't considered newsworthy.

"Believe it. We found another victim found two days ago—that's almost two dozen in three weeks. The FBI is keeping a lid on it, but that won't last much longer."

My gut churned uncomfortably. Upstate New York has had more than its share of serial killers; the press was calling this one the Broken Heart Killer because the victims were all found with their hearts missing. So far, the public had no idea that a demon was to blame.

Reynolds pushed a half-eaten sausage through a puddle of ketchup on his plate. "John Fewkes has just been put on the FBI's most wanted list. First demon master to ever make the list."

I gave a low whistle. "I'm surprised. Ted Roper didn't seem very interested when I tried to talk to him about the sorcery cult a few weeks ago."

Reynolds made a face and slurped his coffee. "Roper is out. Packed up and gone already. Hugo Green is the new Agent in Charge. He's running us ragged, as if we weren't short-handed already. Just what this county needs—another serial killer." He started to say something else, but stopped as the waitress approached.

I remembered Green from the hospital. He and another agent had questioned me the day after it all want down. Reynolds had been there, too, and listened to me lie to them. And he never said a word. We were silent while she refilled his cup, slipped the check in front of him, and sashayed off.

"What were you going to say?" I asked.

He cleared his throat. "You know, my wife thought very highly of you."

I thought he was joking, but his expression was dead serious. Joanne Reynolds had worked in the Human Resources department at the Public Safety Training Facility in Rochester, where I attended the Police Academy. I remembered the tall brunette, but hardly knew her. This was the first time Reynolds had mentioned his wife to me since she'd been murdered by the county's last serial killer, the Night Shark. The sociopathic murderer was eventually revealed as Garlan Russ, a demon master and the only son of 'Mad' Otto Russ, the richest man in Shore Haven.

And if he was to be believed, my father.

He'd revealed that particularly horrific tidbit to me just before I killed him. Another painful memory I would never forget

No doubt John Fewkes and the Nalusa Falaya must be bringing up a lot of painful memories for Reynolds, too.

"She wanted me to hire you out of the Academy," Reynolds told me. "Said you had good test scores, but more than that, she thought you had the right instincts. She was surprised you didn't get picked up by Picston PD. No one was more surprised than Joanne when you took that meter maid job. She nagged me for years to take you away from them."

The taste of ashes filled my mouth. My mother's long and colorful arrest record and Lance's scrapes with the law, uncovered in the background checks, had pretty much tainted my chances at getting a job with Picston PD. A painful memory, one I'd thought I'd forgotten. "I hoped the job would eventually lead to an offer to join the force." Seven years, and I was still waiting.

"Look Mattie," Reynolds leaned forward. "I've been meaning to talk to you about that."

"Yeah, right."

"I'm not kidding," he protested. "This has been in the works for a while. It was Lou's idea, but it was a good one. Lou's been moonlighting for me a few nights a week ever since I got elected. It's wolf patrol—mostly vamp and werewolf calls. After his partner was killed, he wanted to keep his eye on the Fewkes cult. He was determined to bring them down, and so we worked out deal. When his private investigator business started taking off, he brought me the idea to train you to take over wolf patrol. We were going to pitch this to you together, but now..." Reynolds shrugged.

"He's dead," I said. The words hung in the air between us.

"The offer stands, Mattie. You'll have an unmarked patrol car, with a radio and an arsenal in the trunk—taser baton, ketamine dart pistols, riot gear, the works. Your hours will be the same as Lou's—second shift. You'll report directly to me. Special contractor, same deal Lou had. How about it?"

"You're offering me a job?" I couldn't believe what I was hearing. "You've arrested me for murder."

"It wasn't personal, Mattie. Just doing my job."

"Twice," I countered.

"Well, yes, I did." A ghost of a smile played at his lips. "Joanne was a smart cookie—she was right about you. In the last year, I've seen you hold your ground in situations where more seasoned officers would have balked. You're cool under pressure and not queasy about vamps. The Growlers Pub pack likes you."

"I don't know why they would say that," I muttered. "I haven't done the wolves any favors." Kevin was the bartender at Growlers, the were-bar where Rhys and I had recruited volunteers to try and disrupt the summoning of the Nalusa Falaya.

"Don't get me wrong. The wolves will keep you busy, and they can be resentful of authority. It took me years to gain their trust. They respected Lou, but Lou wasn't human. They knew he trusted you."

When I'd attended the Academy, all those years ago, my only goal was to join Picston PD. I wanted it all—the uniform, the patrol car, the brotherhood, the excitement. After all those rejections, I'd buried my feelings deep. I'd never considered the Sheriff's office, but I liked Reynolds, and I knew he liked me. And with Lou gone, I could believe he needed me.

I'd be a real law enforcement officer. *Deputy Blackman* had a good ring to it. I could actually do something to help the lycans and maybe help break up the witch cult. Maybe even find out where Fewkes was hiding. And if I could find Fewkes... "What's the catch?" I asked.

"You'll be walking into a tense situation. The war between witches and lycans is nasty and getting uglier every day. The Penfield cultists have been accused of ambushing pack members when they're alone. And just so you know, one of the demon's recent victims was a werewolf. Their blood is up, and I can't be in two places at once. On one hand, I've got the FBI bent on taking out Fewkes, and on the other, we're on the brink of a blood feud between the lycans and that damned witch cult. Without Lou, I've got no one to handle the lycans."

"I want to be part of the Fewkes investigation." I had no illusions about what the FBI could do against John Fewkes and his cult. Even if they managed to capture him, there was no prison that could hold a sorcerer. I did not believe that there was enough firepower or ketamine in the state to disarm John Fewkes. He would be protected by powerful magic. And what about the Nalusa Falaya? It could evaporate into smoke. How could they possibly stop it?

They would never be able to free Rhys from the spirit tree. I couldn't shake the idea that if the Nalusa Falaya had been imprisoned in the spirit tree once, it could be done again. Someone somewhere had to know how it was done. I was determined to figure it out. I *had* to.

He shook his head. "Not a chance. You're a witness. You are specifically and completely cut out of the loop. Officially, the search for John Fewkes and his demon is the FBI's show now. Agent Green is no dummy; I'll want your word that you will not interfere with their investigation."

"That said," Reynolds continued, "I expect you to keep me informed of any actions and observations that might encounter while on wolf patrol that might be pertinent."

He was giving me a loophole big enough to drive through. Would he keep his word? The Shore Haven vamps considered Sheriff Reynolds a straight-shooter. I didn't have much experience with werewolves, but I believed Reynolds when he said he'd earned their trust. And Lou had worked for him. Lou was good at secrets; there was no real reason to keep his contract with Reynolds quiet—yet he had. I had a hunch there was a lot more depth to Sheriff Reynolds than I gave him credit for.

"Okay, I'm in," I said. "Thank you, sir."

He shook my hand. "Call me Jimbo."

CHAPTER 3

I TRUDGED UP the snow-covered walk to the big old empty house on Empress Street, the fleeting warmth of hot chocolate and waffles already lost to the freezing temperatures. The snow crunched and squealed beneath my boots. Reynolds told me I could start my new job just as soon as I gave notice to the City of Picston. Officially, I had another week of medical leave ahead of me, but I didn't need it. I'd go into work and give my notice tomorrow.

I stepped up onto the porch and froze.

The front door was ajar.

My mind raced, running through any number of scenarios, even as I pushed the door open and stepped into the hall, clutching the empty back brace like a shield in front of me. "Henri, is that you?"

The parlor had been ransacked.

The armoire where Madame Coumlie's journals

were stored had been opened, and the shelves had been emptied. Dozens of the woman's leather-bound journals lay strewn across the carpet. The drawers of her computer desk had been opened—their contents dumped on the floor.

I slipped my shears into my hand. "Blix," I whispered.

My djemon appeared on the top of the armoire. "I await your command."

"Who did this?"

Before he could answer, a robin-sized grey bird flew through the room, calling out, "She's-ear, she's-ear!"

Jinxey.

I gritted my teeth and followed my half-brother's djemon toward the kitchen. Lance was sitting at the kitchen table, eating a peanut butter and jam sandwich, a half-empty bottle of McKenzie Rye whiskey within arm's reach. His eyes were unnaturally bright, his skin pale and sweaty. Deep crow's feet marked the corners of his eyes.

"Hey Matt," he greeted me around a mouthful of peanut butter. He washed down the sandwich with a swallow of rye, straight from the bottle, giving me the hard eye, as if he dared me to say something.

In my memories, Lance is my tan and shaggy-haired hero—the coolest guy I know, with an easy smile and killer dimples. Six months ago, he'd been long and lean, whip hard, and fit. I scarcely recognized him now.

His straw-colored hair had been slicked back and tied into a greasy-looking ponytail. Thick silver bracelets encircled his wrists. His knuckles were bruised and scraped. Beneath the yellow glow of the kitchen light, dark circles sagged below his eyes. Lance was ten years older than me, but he'd aged twenty years since I'd last seen him at Madame Coumlie's funeral. When had his features gotten so hard? Had his expression always been so cynical?

I swallowed a sudden lump in my throat. "You look awful," I said.

He took another swig. "Good to see you, too, kiddo."

"What are you doing here?" I pointed toward the mess in the parlor. "And what the hell is all that about?"

"I came to help you, Matt. I always know when you need me." He jerked his head toward the mess in the parlor. "And as far as I can tell, I got here just in time."

"I'm a grown woman. I don't need your help. And wipe that smirk off your face."

"Slow down there, sis." He kicked out a chair from beneath the table. "Have a seat."

I stayed where I was. This was not my brother. Not the brother I'd grown up with, at any rate. This was a stranger—a gambler in the grip of his addiction.

When he got like this, he reminded me of our mom at her worst—dangerous and unpredictable. I wanted nothing to do with him. "Why did you trash the place?"

He laughed. "You think that was me? It was like that when I walked in. You never were much of a housekeeper. Now come on, sit down."

I curled my hands into fists. "I don't want you here, Lance. Not like this."

He gave me that phony innocent look I knew so well. "Like what?"

"You know what I mean."

He waggled his finger at me. "You should thank me. The front door was wide open when I walked in. No wards set. I thought maybe you'd popped over to the neighbor's, but you didn't come back."

I moved to stand beside the chair. "What wards?"

"The old lady lived alone here for half a century, and never had a break-in. The only people allowed to enter this house are *allowed* to enter this house through the wards."

I knew I'd locked the door when I'd left. "What do you know about wards, Lance?"

"Like I told you at the funeral, I knew her. Been coming to her for years. I didn't know we were related or anything, but I could feel the wards every time I came to visit. It was like this house was an extension of Celeste Coumlie. But not today. When I walked in today, they were gone. This house is dead."

I considered all the people and other creatures that had traipsed through the house over the past several months. Demons, Vampires. Dreamspiders. Maybe Lance was right. Had the wards had died with her? It didn't matter. I'd locked the door when I'd left, I was sure of it. Lance had broken in, and was now trying to change the subject.

"I don't have any money," I said. "What do you want?

"Since when do I need a reason to come and visit my daughter and my kid sister?"

"You told Violet and me that you were going to rehab. Violet won't let you see Mina like this, and I don't blame her." Lance had practically raised me—I hated seeing him like this. "You're still gambling, I can always tell."

"You're totally unprotected, here, Matt. That mage boyfriend of yours should have taken care of it for you. Where is Rhys, anyway?"

I flinched, as if from a blow.

Of course he misunderstood my reaction.

"Ah, sorry Matt. I told you he wasn't the right guy for you. Don't worry, I know a woman--." His gaze met mine. "She renewed the house wards for Madame Coumlie every year."

"I don't care about that. We haven't heard from you in months, and you show up looking like hell. What's going on, Lance?"

A rueful look passed over his features. "That is a very long story for another day. Right now, a hot shower and a warm bed would do me fine. A place to stay for a few days would be nice. Been sleeping rough the last couple nights." He rubbed his chest. "How about it, Matt? I'm near done in."

I recognized the old worn jean jacket sitting on the back of his chair. Lance always travelled light. After nearly freezing my ears off today, I couldn't very well turn my brother out on a night like this.

"Tell me why you're here."

The slow grin I knew so well reached his eyes this time, and the old Lance I knew and loved was right there again.

"All in good time. I'm too tired to fight. You're gonna have to wait until breakfast. "

❦

The sound of the washing machine going in the basement woke me the next morning. The aroma of fresh-brewed coffee floated up the stairs and for half a minute, Rhys was downstairs making breakfast, same as always.

Then I remembered.

The crushing blow of loss sent my back into a spasm. That was Lance downstairs, not Rhys.

I rolled into a fetal position, and waited for the

physical and mental anguish to pass. After pulling on an old pair of jeans and a hooded sweatshirt, I headed downstairs. My great grandmother's journals still lay in a scattered pile on the floor of the parlor.

I should really clean this up before I go into work and turn in my resignation. Better yet, get Lance to do it. It was *his* mess, not mine. And he'd promised me an explanation.

But first, coffee.

Lance was seated at the kitchen table with his back turned to me, wearing a pair of Henri's flannel pajama bottoms, the contents of my first aid kit scattered across the table in front of him. A shamrock tattoo on his left shoulder blade was something I hadn't seen before. His arms had also been inked in full-color sleeves to the wrist. A spread of playing cards in clubs and spades on the right, red diamonds and hearts on the left.

"Morning," I mumbled, making a beeline for the gurgling Mr. Coffee. Lance was drinking out of my Red Sonja coffee mug. It *would* be petty of me to demand it back, but Rhys had given it to me. The Spirit Festival cup was clean, but I hated that cup. Designed by this summer's Spirit Festival chairman Enzo Obote, the cup bore an artist's conception of Shore Haven after the new marina was built and the downtown area gentrified with fancy hotels and shopping malls. *Beverly Hills East,* they called it. Designed by Mad

Otto Russ and his rich investor cronies as a weekend getaway destination for the elite. The arrogant motto, *Spirit of the Future*, ticked me off every time I thought about it. Already, half the stores in Shore Haven had sold out to Mad Otto's consortium and moved on.

I topped the cup with a healthy splash of milk and took a slurp.

Aaah. In spite of the cup, the first sip of the day was always the best.

A furtive movement from Lance caught my attention. He held his hand to his bare chest, only partially covering what looked like a fresh tattoo. The skin looked red and angry.

"That looks infected," I said. "Let me see."

"Not a chance. I know what I'm doing."

Lance made as if to stand, but I shoved him back into his chair. I was surprised at his lack of resistance. "I'm not asking, I'm telling. Show me."

When he removed his hand, I hissed at the sight.

The design of the tattoo was immediately recognizable as one of the cards in Madame Coumlie's tarot deck—the *Wheel of Fortune* card. Primitive, but iconic—a wheel with twelve spokes, spinning among the clouds, suspended between the lands of the living and the dead. A catbird, looking very much like Jinxey perched on the top portion of the wheel. The colors were vivid; bright oranges, turquoise, and yellow, edged in blue-black ink. But the tattoo had not merely been inked; the image had been *carved* into his skin, scarring it. It must have been done quite some time ago, because nearly all the scars had healed. All except for a raised and angry mass in the center of the wheel. Lance flinched when I ran my thumb across the hard, compact lump.

"There's something in there," I said. "A foreign body of some sort. It's infected."

"No, its fine," he answered, pushing me away. His cheeks were ruddy, his forehead glistened with sweat. "I know what I'm doing. It's just taking a while to heal, that's all."

"It smells bad, Lance. It's gotta come out."

He daubed antibiotic ointment over the worst of it, and held the clean bandage pad over the wound. "Why don't you make yourself useful and help me wrap this thing up?" At the base of each of his wrists was an image of a joker in fool's garb. Black on the right, red on the left.

Silently, I took the roll of gauze from him and wrapped it around his chest. I had to bite my lips together to keep from saying anything. When I finished, I tossed the gauze and scissors onto the table.

He wiped his face on the dishtowel. "It's a foreign body implant, okay? As it happens, infection is part of the process. Eventually, the body will build up granuloma tissue around it, and it will become part of me."

"Oh cripes. Isn't the ink enough?" I frowned. "What kind of foreign body?"

"Something I can't afford to lose." He sighed. "Now, how about a splash of coffee for your dear old brother, or are you going to hog the whole pot?"

I had his cup refilled before he got the words out. Part of it was waitress instinct, but I'd always been eager to please Lance. As a kid, I'd worshipped him—in my eyes, he could do no wrong.

But those days were past. As much as I loved him, Lance loved gambling more than his wife, his daughter, or, well, anything. It was an addiction he didn't want to be cured of. And now there was something seriously wrong with him—it wasn't just his grey lifeline that made me afraid for him.

I sat down at the table. "What's going on, Lance? I mean, really. No bullshit."

He set the cup down. "Where is Madame Coumlie's tarot deck?"

"That's why you came back?" I nodded toward the mess in the parlor. "That's why you tore her room apart? You thought you'd just come in here and take it?" I felt sick to my stomach. This stranger hardly resembled the man who'd raised me. I didn't trust him. I chewed my lip, wishing more than anything that Rhys was here.

"I told you I did not do that. Look Matt, it's just an old deck of tarot cards. We both know you don't buy into the fortune teller bit. Why not just give it to me?"

"They're mine. They're my legacy. She left them to me, Lance."

"So let me borrow them."

"What happened to you?" There was something seriously wrong with his lifeline. "Why do you want them?"

"Don't you trust me?" Suddenly serious, he shook his head. "I'm not going to sell them, if that's what you think."

Carved of hippopotamus teeth, there were eighteen rectangular tiles, each less than three inches long and an inch wide. Rhys, who would know, told me the cards were very old. He thought they could be older than any other known cards. Museum quality, he said. But I didn't care about that. I couldn't shake the feeling that if I gave Lance the cards, I'd never see him again.

"I don't know where they are." Of course I knew exactly where they were. All wrapped up in an orange scarf and stashed behind the secret drawer in the parlor. "This is pointless," I said, and headed for the parlor.

"What? Come on. Don't be that way, Matt. They're of no use to you." He followed me to the parlor and stood in the doorway, watching as I gathered up the leather-bound journals and re-shelved them into the armoire.

I glared at him. "I'm not having this conversation

with you right now Lance. I've got--." A boyfriend to rescue. A blood feud to stop. An immortal sorcerer to kill. And a demon to banish. A chill swept through me, as I remembered my failure to banish the Nalusa Falaya in the graveyard. "Places to go." I cleared my throat. "Things to do."

Don't forget the demon.

"I'll go with you." He seemed to get the hint and started picking up the journals, handing them to me.

"You can't. I'm going to turn in my notice--." I suddenly remembered that Charlie and I had a house to clear of spirits today. I was supposed to pick him up at noon. I'd better get going.

He frowned. "You're quitting? You love that stupid job."

"It's not stupid. But as it happens, Sheriff Reynolds made me a better offer." I couldn't help but gloat a little. "You're looking at Monroe County's newest Deputy."

"Cop groupie," he sneered. "You always were a sucker for the uniform. The law is not your friend Matt. Or have you forgotten how it is for us in this town?"

"Shut up. You don't know anything." That was his addiction talking. Always the victim; never take responsibility for his own actions. I'd forgotten how much I hated him like this. I wanted to yell at him. To hug him. To shake him and make him stop. He was in such bad shape, though. I couldn't ask him to leave. I shoved the last armful of journals into the armoire and slammed the doors shut.

"You think you can just--."

A curled black feather drifted to the floor.

A raven's feather.

I didn't say a word. I snatched up my leather jacket from the coat tree and swept out the door. Lucky for me, Trusty Rusty fired up on the first try, and I was out of there before Lance could get his shoes on.

CHAPTER 4

MY BOSS, MIKE, scarcely blinked when I told him I'd accepted a job at the Sheriff's department. He even waived my two-week notice, saying the other members of the team would appreciate the extra hours.

"I know how much you've been wanting this," was all he said, when I handed him my badge and ticket book. "Guess your luck has finally turned."

"It wasn't luck, Mike. I'm the right person for the job." It came out sharper than I intended.

He nodded. "Of course. I get it. Circumstances have changed. No hard feelings, eh?"

Mike and I had been close, once. Tight. Had it been so long ago? Seemed like it. We hardly knew each other anymore. The barriers between us hadn't been there a year ago. I know he felt it too.

And that was it. Seven years of my life in that job, and I walked out of Pictson City Hall and down the wide front steps to my car, feeling hollow.

Everything was changing. One ten-minute conversation with my boss, and a seven-year chapter of my life was over—summed up in the receding reflection in Trusty Rusty's rear-view mirror as I drove away—toward Shore Haven, where the not-yet-built new marina already cast a giant shadow over the familiar small town I'd grown up in.

I could almost hear the sound of a great iron door slamming behind me. Parking Control represented the last shreds of my old life. It hadn't exactly been the life I imagined for myself, but I was used to it. I'd crossed a threshold.

Of course I'd changed too. I was a far different person now than I'd been when I'd started working for Mike. I was more experienced. I'd seen things—things Morta had shown me that no one else could or would ever see. Done things I couldn't undo. As hard as I'd resisted becoming the Hand of Fate, I had to admit that it was part of who I was now, too. No doubt that being sworn in as an officer of the law would change me even more

My closest friends now were Blix, Rhys, Neldene, and Charlie. A djemon, a djenie, a vamp, and Morta's psychopomp. The very idea was mind-boggling. Not one of them had ever questioned my character or given me any reason to think they didn't have my back. I trusted them with my life, and I knew they trusted me. So strange that I couldn't say the same about Mike or any of the other people in Parking Control.

I tried not to let it bother me.

I drove into the parking lot at the Shore Happy Motor Court next to the Heavenly Shores Amusement Park. The dilapidated cabins looked even sadder under a layer of clean white snow, until I reached the end of the row, where Charlie Crimmer's neat brown and white cottage sat.

I was an hour early, but I knew he'd be home. Charlie didn't drive and we had an appointment to go clear a haunted house. The house clearing business had started as a side job, but the extra cash was good for both of us. With the park closed up for the winter, his hours as a security guard had been cut in half.

He welcomed me with true warmth; his leathery brown wrinkles alight with pleasure. "Come in, come in, girlie. Glad to see you're back on yer feet." Charlie already knew most of the details of what had happened on the night of the ritual. I'd called him from the hospital and given him the gist of what had happened.

While Charlie fussed in the kitchen, making a fresh pot of coffee, his djemon, Annie, watched her master's every move from her dog bed next to Charlie's worn recliner. Annie's form is that of a pterodactyl, yet somehow, she seemed perfectly at home amid the clutter of artifacts, hand-woven rugs and bundles of herbs hanging from the rafters of the ancient shaman's living room.

"Rhys is still alive, Charlie." I slipped out of my leather jacket and boots and went to stand in front of his electric fireplace. The flames were fake, but the heat felt good. "I went to the ritual site yesterday," I began. "I swear I felt his presence trapped inside the spirit tree."

Charlie had been the one who had identified the Nalusa Falaya as the demon imprisoned in the spirit tree that John Fewkes intended to free.

"Not for long," he answered. "Every part of that tree is poison. It sapped the Nalusa Falaya's immortal strength, but Rhys is not immortal—it will kill him."

I felt as if I'd been sucker-punched. "But it's just a tree..."

"No. Not a tree. A vile thing created by the People as a measure of last resort. Many of The People sacrificed themselves to awaken it. It is said to feed upon the spirit of its victims over centuries. For the People, it was an ugly thing; best forgotten."

My gorge rose. I crossed to the sofa and sank to the cushions. "There's got to be a way to open that tree. Can't we just cut it down? Or burn it."

"I know that cutting down the tree or burning it will kill the mage."

I accepted the cup of hot coffee from Charlie with trembling hands. The heady aroma of fresh-brewed coffee comforted me. "There's got to be a way to get him out of there. You must know something."

Charlie took a seat in his weathered recliner. "It happened before my time. The Elders would not speak of it."

"I can't just leave him there, Charlie."

Charlie settled into his recliner, his hand absently stroking Annie's head on his knee. "You witnessed the ritual. What did the sorcerer say to open the tree?"

I thought back to that horrible night. "We couldn't hear anything. The coven was already inside a ritual circle when we got there; the sounds were muffled. If I hadn't banished Fewkes's demon, the Nalusa Falaya might have been trapped in the circle, instead of—." I fought to control my emotions.

"Liddy Fewkes used dozens of wooden dolls, each with a soul bound inside. The Nalusa Falaya ate every one. Even if I'd heard the spell, I swore an oath to Morta to protect the dead. My oath to Morta forbids me from ever exploiting souls—not even to open the tree. There's got to be another way. How did Fewkes even learn about the tree?"

"That is a question for John Fewkes, girlie."

I told Charlie about how the Nalusa Falaya had demanded "the muse" and how the raven had chased Blix and me into one of the crypts. "I think maybe the

Nalusa Falaya tricked John Fewkes. I think maybe the sorcerer is trapped in raven form. They had me trapped for hours, and Fewkes never changed out of bird form." I thought about it. "And they both left together." It was almost as if Fewkes answered to the demon.

"The sorcerer is not the problem," Charlie said. "You've got to find a way to put the Nalusa Falaya back in the spirit tree. Nothing else will stop the killing."

Impossible. There were just too many problems for one person to solve. "How long does Rhys have, Charlie? I mean, before the tree kills him?"

The old man grunted. "No way to know. He'll probably go mad first. Best not to dwell on it."

I bit back a retort. Charlie was pragmatic, not cruel. He wasn't trying to be heartless—he was trying to help me come to terms with a reality I didn't want to accept.

"I love him." I growled over the words. "I can't walk away. I've *got* to get him out of there. I've just got to."

"Fewkes, then." Charlie nodded. "You'll be making a deal with the devil, but he's the only one with the answers you want and the power to do something about it."

Yeah. Like that was going to happen. "I'd probably have a better chance with Blix."

When it came right down to it, my little djemon was a wiz with my laptop. He'd long since graduated from the Speak 'n Read tablet to the archives of international research libraries. Maybe he could find something.

"What is this thing about the muse?"

I shook my head. "I have no idea. I don't know if he meant music, or a *real* Muse. It seemed to me like he thought I could get what he wanted and give it to him." I sipped my coffee. "You said your clansmen imprisoned the Nalusa Falaya in the spirit tree. Is there anything about a Muse that was part of the ritual?"

Charlie frowned. "Muse is a white man's word. It is not part of the Senequois language. The demon could not have learned that word from the People."

"Rats. I was hoping you knew." Another dead end.

The client's house was a sixty year old, split-level ranch in Henrietta. The owner had died in the house, and the new owners were convinced it was haunted. There was not much for me to do at the client's house— no pesky djinn or djemons banish, so while Charlie cleared the house with his herbs and chanting, I set Blix to work on my laptop.

Actually, I hadn't had much use for it, lately. Blix started out using my laptop as a learning tool, but he'd become quite the expert in a very short time. Better and faster than me.

"I need you to find out everything you can about spirit trees, Blix. How they're made, how to open them. Everything. Rumors, facts, local legends, whatever."

Blix licked his lips, a sure sign of excitement.

"And you might as well look into the history of the Senequois People. It must have been written down at some point. And anything you can about the Penfield family, too."

"Rhys was documenting the history of the Senequois and other local tribes as part of his research," Blix informed me. "He may have made notes."

"Good thinking," I agreed. Mystic Properties had been locked up for weeks. Rhys had spent the past year researching the indigenous people of the Finger Lakes region. *Oh Rhys.* "Don't make a mess of it, though."

Blix sat up straighter and flicked his ears back. "No *proper* djemon would ever leave evidence of its presence."

"That goes for unauthorized internet access as well." Like any other djemon, Blix could traverse different astral planes—no lock or wall on the physical plane was a barrier to him. The Internet was a different matter. Law enforcement agencies regularly troll the internet, tracking certain keywords and queries as part of their anti-terrorism activities. Keywords like *demon*, *immortal*, and *ritual* were probably high on the list. I paused, debating whether to set my djemon on such a task. I phrased the command carefully. "Blix I need to know how to kill an immortal demon, but I don't want anyone to be able to track that kind of a search. Can you do it?"

"I do not need the internet to answer that question," Blix replied. "Djemons are not alive in the human sense; therefore, they cannot be killed. They may only be contained or banished from a place or time. You refer to the Nalusa Falaya as a demon, but he is not like Annie or I. He is an elemental spirit who answers to no master. Very unpredictable and dangerous. In your quest to rescue Rhys, I fear that your feelings for him are stronger than your sense of self preservation."

"Thank you Blix," I answered. "That's so sweet of you to worry about me."

"My future depends on your survival."

"Yeah." I sighed. My bad, thinking that Blix or any djemon possessed human emotions. "Thanks for the reminder."

"I live to serve, Mistress."

CHAPTER 5

AFTER CLEARING THE client's house, I dropped Charlie off at his place and drove to downtown Rochester to fill out the requisite paperwork at the Sheriff's office before starting the new job.

There was no public swearing in ceremony, but Sheriff Reynolds was there. A strange sense of déjà-vu washed over me as I repeated the oath, which reminded me so much of my pledge to Morta. If anything, this new vow, which I'd dreamed of taking since I was a young girl, reaffirmed my commitment as Morta's Hand.

"I, Matilda Blackman, affirm that I will support the Constitution of the United States,
the Constitution of the State of New York, and
Monroe County Code, and all the laws thereof,
and that I will faithfully discharge my duties in

*accordance with the lawful policies and procedures
of the Monroe County Sheriff's Office.
In reverence for the law, I shall conduct my duties in
good faith, with honesty, courage, and justice,
to the best of my ability. In so doing I shall build the
people's trust and confidence in my position.
I shall never betray them by willfully abusing my
powers, authority or knowledge."*

As I spoke the final words, the weight of my new obligation to uphold the laws of the living settled comfortably alongside Morta's covenant to protect the dead. It felt right.

After the paperwork was signed, Sheriff Reynolds shook my hand, and welcomed me to the department, as did Field Training Officer, Alma Waters. Waters, a seasoned deputy some ten years older than me, had been with the Monroe County Sheriff's department since before Reynolds had been elected. She took her responsibilities for mentoring new recruits through the eight-week probationary period seriously. Given that this was my first night on the street, she'd be riding shotgun until she felt I was ready to go it alone.

At six feet and change, Waters was two hundred pounds of solid muscle clothed in a plain brown wrapper. Her rolling bulldog gait reflected competence, confidence, and intensity. I was more than a little intimidated. I followed her into the garage beneath the building where the sheriff's department vehicles were parked. "First of all, there are no stupid questions," she began. "If you don't know, ask. That's what I'm here for."

At the end of a row of gleaming patrol cars, she stopped in front of a Subaru Forrester with a matte black paint job. The faint scent of engine oil tickled my nose.

"Here's your ride. It's not regulation, but Scali insisted."

I ran my hand across the hood, noting the clots of dried mud and salt coating the wheel wells. I could almost feel Lou's ghost at my shoulder, saying, *in the winter, a dirty car is less noticeable than a clean one.* The interior was spotless. "He loved Subarus. Safest car on the road, he said. The perfect surveillance car."

Waters hesitated, as if she wanted to say something.

"What?" I said.

"Jimbo tells me you'll be riding solo."

"Yeah." A little bubble of pride swelled within me.

"Scali used his cell phone to call for back up; not that he ever did, that I recall. There's no radio in the vehicle. We can get one installed, if you want."

Lou would never call for human backup. He didn't want anyone else to get hurt on his watch, as he blamed himself for his partner's death. This was wolf patrol. A call for backup was like asking your fellow officer to commit suicide. If Lou could work without a human net, so could I.

"I'll be fine." And I meant it. This was it. The keys were in the ignition, waiting for me. This was my patrol car. An adrenaline drumbeat echoed through me. "I've got this."

Waters smirked. "Don't be stupid, rookie. It'll get you killed out there. Or worse, get one of us killed when you get in over your head and call for backup."

I met her hard expression with one of my own. "Respect is everything to weres. If I show up in a radio unit, it will make me look weak. I might as well wear the uniform."

Given that I was wearing my scratched up old leathers and Waters was wearing a uniform that was so freshly pressed, I could smell the starch in her collar, I counted myself lucky that she didn't backhand me half-way across the garage.

"Listen up, Blackman, 'cause I'm only going to say this once." She took a step closer, her hands on her hips. "Wolf patrol is like playing Russian roulette with only one empty chamber. If you don't get bit, you're gonna get killed. You want to end up like Scali?"

She was trying to scare me. "It wasn't werewolves that killed Lou," I said. When it came to things that scared me, lycans didn't even make my top-ten list.

"That doesn't mean I'm wrong." She sniffed, unimpressed. "Scali's death should have convinced the Sheriff that wolf patrol is a bad idea."

My cheeks grew warm. Maybe she was just playing

bad cop. Or maybe this was the kind of welcome speech she gave all the new recruits—a way to test their mettle and commitment. It didn't matter—her mind was made up, and I was going to be a dim-witted rookie until she decided otherwise. She sounded like Master Foo and his constant admonitions to focus. Only this wasn't Qhua Bei practice, or sitting stakeout with Lou anymore. This was the real thing.

That didn't mean I was going to let her walk all over me.

"Look, I appreciate the warning, but the blood feud between the Lycans and the witches is about to erupt. I was Lou's apprentice, and the local pack asked for me specifically. The Sheriff thinks I'm ready, and there's nobody else, so let's quit arguing and get on with it—um, Ma'am."

Without either of us giving in, the tension eased between us. "We are the light in the darkness, Blackman. Protectors of the innocent."

Ironic that my oath to Morta was so similar. "I know that," I answered.

"Your friend Scali kept a low profile around here. I can't say I knew him well, but his loss has affected all of us. Everyone is jumpy. You really think you can handle a pack of enraged werewolves all by yourself?"

The little bubble of pride swelled up within me again. "I'm the best person for this job."

"That's not saying much, Deputy." She gave me a

wry smile. "There are more than wolves to worry about out there."

"Yes, there is," I agreed. "Even this rookie knows that."

She pressed her lips together for a beat. "Alright, let's roll," she said. She walked around to the passenger door and got in.

I settled in behind the wheel, fastened my seatbelt, and fired up the engine, but Waters wasn't done yet.

"Always, always know where you are," Waters admonished. "This isn't Shore Haven. Keep your head on a swivel and make note of every mile marker and intersection. A lot of new officers have a hard time learning the layout of the county. Drive around on your off days and get to know every corner of it until you know it like the back of your hand. Scali did. Learn which roads get plowed and which don't. You don't want to be dispatched on a hot call and have to look it up on a map."

I nodded. I knew the county better than most, but she was right. "Good suggestion." I put the car in gear and cruised out of the parking garage.

"Head south," Waters ordered. "We'll start in Perinton, then head west through Mendon, Rush and Wheatland, then north through Riga and Ogden to Hamlin. There's diner in Greece I like. Ever eat at the Potato Shack?"

"Can't say I get out there much." I turned south on

Henrietta Road.

The first call of the night took us out to the village of Honeoye Falls, for a domestic problem—a single mother, Maggie Petteri, who had came home from work to find a vampire feeding on her sixteen-year-old daughter. The woman claimed she'd managed to subdue the vamp and we needed to come pick him up.

When Waters and I arrived, we could hear someone screaming from inside the house. A group of curious neighbors had gathered in the driveway. While Waters handled the spectators, I went inside to assess the situation. The so-called vamp turned out to be the girl's seventeen year-old boyfriend. Somehow, the mother had managed to restrain the bare-chested teenager with electrical cords and duct tape, while the hysterical daughter flailed and ranted that her mother had gone bat-crap crazy.

Mrs. Petteri glared at me. "What took you so long?"

I showed her my badge. "Deputy Blackman, Ma'am. What's going on here?"

"She's killing Greg," the daughter announced. She was wearing nothing but a thin tank top and a pair of pink sweatpants. A couple of large hickeys bloomed bright red and purple on her neck.

"Don't be ridiculous, Ellie. He's already dead. I know my rights, Deputy." Her eyes shone with conviction. "He attacked my daughter. I had to protect her."

On the floor, Greg, the supposed vampire, began to squirm. Duct tape wouldn't hold a normal vamp—this Goth kid was no vampire. I checked him to make sure he could breathe. On closer inspection, Greg was also sporting several human bite marks.

"I shouldn't have to do your job for you, officer," Ellie's mother complained. "Get him out of here."

"He's not a vampire, Ma'am." I had to bite the inside of my cheek to keep a straight face when I told her. I grabbed a corner of the duct tape covering Greg's mouth and ripped it off.

"I told her I'm no vamper, but she wouldn't listen. Cut me loose. I wanna press charges against the both of 'em. False imprisonment." He glared at Ellie. "Torture."

Suddenly the girl had nothing to say.

A frown of doubt flickered across Mrs. Petteri's face, and "How can you be so sure?"

I showed her the marks on Glen's neck and chest. "Those are love bites, not fang marks. I think maybe Ellie and Glen were, um..."

"She made me to do it!" Glen nodded vigorously. "Cut me loose!"

I pointed at him. "Settle down, you. You're in enough trouble already."

Mrs. Petteri stiffened, her fists clenched. "Hickeys. Are you sure?"

"Yes Ma'am. The boy has them, too."

At that point, Ellie burst into tears and ran upstairs. "I can't believe she lied to me," Mrs. Petteri murmured. "I don't like that boy. I don't care if he's a vampire or not, I don't want him in my house."

Now that she was certain that Greg wasn't a vampire, she decided not to press charges. Once Waters and I got Greg untied, he calmed down and fifteen minutes later, we dropped him off at his parent's house with a warning.

I cleared the call—my first on wolf patrol. I was a real deputy.

"If I was a betting woman—which I'm not," Waters observed. "I'd bet this won't be the last time we get called to break up Greg and Ellie." She shook her head. "Love is wasted on the young."

"Maybe." I was no teenager, but every time I thought of Rhys my heart hurt. The thought of having him so close and yet so impossible to reach was a scratch I couldn't itch. A missing part of me. "I'm not so sure it gets any easier with age."

"It's a simple thing," Waters said. "Wanting someone to love and be loved by. We all want it. You'd think that after all this time, we'd have figured out to do it without the drama."

There was a yearning in her voice. "That sounds like the voice of experience."

She sniffed. "Love and pain are universal. It connects us all."

"No matter who we are or where we come from," I agreed.

At that moment, our eyes met, and the tension in the car dissipated. I got the impression that when she was off-duty, Waters was not at all the drill sergeant she appeared to be on the job.

"Eyes on the road, Blackman," she said.

"I got it." I eased the car back into my lane.

"I hear you were hell on wheels in your meter maid days."

"Hey that's not fair. I've never crashed a Subaru."

"It's only your first day," she answered.

❧

Our last call of the night was a hit-and-run accident in Penfield, on Five-Mile Line Road, just half a mile from Growlers Pub. A late-model Chevy Silverado had been run off the road into a tree. The 911 caller said witnesses pulled the unconscious driver out, and then fled when he began to shift.

The victim lay unconscious on the side of the road, his shoes and torn clothes scattered in the road. A pulse raced at his neck. Steam wafted off his hot bare skin. His fingernails were caked with blood and dirt. "It's a were, all right," I told Waters, who was searching the truck. "Looks like he shifted to wolf and back too quickly. I'm sure he'll be out for a while."

"Dart him and we'll both be sure."

I bit back my argument. Didn't seem right to add insult to the victim's injury, but ketamine would keep both us and the lycan safe while we transported him to lockup. "Yes Ma'am."

I got out the dart pistol and shot the helpless guy in the butt. He didn't even flinch.

She rifled through his torn clothes. "No registration in the truck, and I don't see a wallet. You recognize him?"

I flashed the light in his eyes. "I don't think so." He wasn't in any condition to cause us harm, but Waters made me use the silver-plated steel cuffs on his wrists and ankles before I read him his rights. In Monroe County, any lycan caught after dark without identification is taken into custody and held without charges until his identity was verified.

Together, we hoisted the unconscious victim into the back of the Subaru. Ambulances are never called for werewolves. No hospital would ever accept such a dangerous creature. Weres have a powerfully regenerative constitution. Either they recover rapidly, or, in the case of catastrophic trauma, like a silver bullet through the heart or brain, they die. It bugged me that we were required to arrest the victim and lock him up.

After booking the still unconscious werewolf, Waters went off shift, and I drove out to Growlers Pub with a photo of the unidentified victim in my cell phone. It was after midnight when I pulled into the parking lot.

Inside, the heavy beat of the Rolling Stones should have had everyone grooving to the beat, but instead, an itching buzz of agitated werewolf pheromones, called weremones, reached me as soon as I walked in. Someone pulled the plug on the jukebox. Everyone turned to look at me. A whisper went through the crowd. I heard Lou's name mentioned.

I spotted Kevin behind the bar, looking tense.

"What's going on, Kev?" I asked.

"Another pack member has been killed," he said. "That's three dead in as many weeks. Now that the witches have their pet smoke demon, they're targeting lycans. Those damn cultists are stalking us and nobody cares."

"I do," I said. Having seen firsthand how badly lycans were treated, I hated it. "The Feds are doing everything they can to catch John Fewkes," I said, but it rang hollow. "That's why there's a voluntary curfew--."

Garvey Hays cut me off. "Because of him, they're punishing us! Those cultists are a bunch of racist bigots, and they always have been. We're the ones being attacked. I've had my tires slashed and rocks thrown through my windows. And tonight, some jerk tried to run me off the road."

The blood feud between the Penfield witch cult

and the Penfield packs was an open secret, and had been going on for years. Months ago, Lou had told me about a restraining order issued against the cult, ordering members to stay more than 200 feet away from Growlers Pub and its patrons. The bar was supposed to be off limits to the witch cult.

"I'm scared to go anywhere alone," said Nixie, one of the barmaids. The crowd murmured their agreement.

"Why the sudden escalation in hostilities," I asked. "Why would the Nalusa Falaya be killing werewolves?"

"Fewkes is ordering him to so, obviously."

I didn't see who'd spoken, but everyone in the room seemed to agree.

Kevin came out from behind the bar. "In their eyes, we're sub-human. Lepers. They don't believe we have a right to live—at least not in 'their' county. They throw dead animals on our lawns, harass our employers, they even get people to picket our businesses. This campaign of harassment has gotten worse over the years, but since they've got that smoke demon on their side, there's no reason for them to stop until they've killed us all."

"And now they're accusing us of stealing from them," said Kevin's girlfriend, Belinda. She slid a crudely drawn wanted posted across the bar. A picture of a wolf with the eyes crossed out. Beneath the drawing, the words, *GIVE IT BACK OR MORE WILL DIE,* was scrawled.

"Like we'd give a rat's ass about anything that belonged to one of them. None of us were even there that night."

Except for Kevin. I caught his gaze. "What do they think you took?"

"A book," Belinda answered. "His sister's."

"I give you my word, Mattie," Kevin assured me. "No one in this bar has ever taken as much as a wooden nickel from any of them. If one of us did, every lycan in the bar would know about it. To us, spellcrafters have a distinctive odor. Their magic reeks of it. If any of us were to come in contact with a witch's grimoire, the rest of us would smell it. It was probably one of their own cult members took it."

The temperature in the room jumped up a couple of degrees.

"We can't touch them, but they come into our territory all the time."

"The FBI isn't doing anything."

"We should have the right to protect ourselves..."

They were psyching themselves up onto a mob. *Or a hunting pack.*

Nothing I could say would change the raw deal that werewolves faced every day, or their understandable lack of trust in law enforcement, and they certainly didn't want me to offer them platitudes about how everything would work out fine.

I needed to divert their attention to something else.

I held up my cell phone with the picture I'd snapped of the unconscious John Were-Doe I'd picked up earlier. "Anybody know this guy?"

Several of the lycans nodded. "He's a regular," Kevin said.

"That's Terry VanSandt." Nixie added. "He's a bow hunting guide and outfitter. He runs pack mules for rich clients who want to rough it in Finger Lakes National Park."

The park was located near Watkins Glen, about eighty miles south of Rochester. "What is he doing up here?"

"His parents live in Webster."

I slipped my phone back into the pocket of my leather jacket. "I just booked him into county lock-up. He didn't have any identification on him."

"That's not cool, Mattie." Kevin explained that Lou always brought injured lycanthropes to Growlers. "We take care of our own."

"Today was my first day on the job." I explained about the accident. "I had a trainer riding shotgun to make sure I followed procedure. Next time I'll know."

Nixie rolled her eyes. "Yeah, right."

I didn't appreciate her cynicism, but I understood it. Acquired Lycanthropy Syndrome wasn't for sissies.

Most of the regulars at Growlers had been infected while serving in the Middle East; the virus had been released as a chemical warfare agent by terrorists. Once infected, they'd been separated from the military and stripped of many of their basic human rights. Discrimination made it tough for many of them to find jobs. Most took a dim view of law enforcement. Lou Scali had been the only wolf patrol they'd ever known. I'd have to earn their trust.

"Look, I checked in on him at the end of my shift, when I finished up the paperwork. He looked like he was coming around. They'll probably release him into your custody, if I'm there too."

The crowd parted for a tall, dark and dangerous-looking guy in his mid-thirties, with a distinctive white streak in his shaggy dark hair. "I'll go."

Kevin introduced him as Trey Halliday, the Penfield pack's Beta.

The white streak in his hair was echoed in a white scar through his right eyebrow, giving him a rakish look. No way would VanSandt be released to his custody unless I was there to vouch for him. The guy's well-worn leathers and gentle voice stirred something in me—something quickly smothered by a sharp pang of guilt. Something about him reminded me a little of Rhys.

We walked across the crusty, hard-packed snow of the parking lot, our boots squeaking on a layer of freshly-fallen dry powder.

"So you're the new Lou?"

"Yep—well, no. Not exactly. There's no one like Lou." I fought to swallow the sudden catch in my throat. *He was one of a kind.*

"Your shift is over, Deputy. Why come all the way out here?"

The street lights along the perimeter of the parking lot flickered in a sudden gust of wind. The cold cut through my jacket like it was tissue paper. "Your friend was the victim of a hit and run. While he was out cold, I hit him with a dose of ketamine. Then I put him in silver wrist and leg irons for transport, and when I got to the station, I had to watch two officers dump him into a cage—buck naked and unconscious. I felt bad about it. I thought somebody ought to know where he was." I stopped beside the Subaru, my throat dry. I cut a brief glance at Halliday. "Hop in; I'll bring you both back."

When he smiled, character lines deepened at the corners of his dark eyes. In spite of his tough guy appearance, he had a good face. A kind face. Tough, yeah—but there was humor there, too. "Go home, Deputy. You look beat. I know my way around the county lock-up," he said. "Been there many times."

"No offense, but no one is going to release a lycan into your custody at this hour."

He grinned. "I suppose you'd think so." He reached

into his jacket, pulled out his badge, and handed it to me.

Chief Treyson Halliday, Penfield Fire Department.

"Oh." It had been a long day. "I guess I'll leave you to it, then."

"Marla and Sam on duty tonight?"

I nodded, feeling like a total noob. "Um, Yeah."

"Hey kid," Trey caught my door as I slipped in behind the wheel. "For what it's worth, Terry has never been in any kind of trouble—never been arrested. When he comes to—well, let's just say that it was a good thing you did, coming out here to let us know." He squinted against a gust of wind-blown powdered snow. "This disease robs us of our humanity in the most devastating ways possible. It strips us of everything that really matters—lovers, kids, families— no one is spared. Even our citizenship is revoked. The only thing lycanthropy can't touch is our community— our pack. The pack connects us all."

In my somewhat limited experience, lycans were clannish and excitable. What Trey implied was something more powerful. That someone so tough and hardened by experience would have a hitch in his voice when he said pack made me like him even more.

"Terry is pack, you understand? He's going to wake up on my couch tomorrow instead of a cage."

I nodded. "Got it." And with those words—and for the second time that day—I knew I'd just sworn an oath to serve and protect pack to the very best of my ability. Settled in between the oaths to support the living and the dead, I didn't have much wiggle room, but the lycans were welcome to it. They weren't looking for a leg up, just even footing.

CHAPTER 6

I STEPPED OUT of the shower to the sound of female laughter coming from downstairs. I couldn't hear what my brother was saying, but he must've been charming the pants off them, because there were definitely two women laughing.

The sound put my teeth on edge. I didn't like that he'd brought them into the house without asking—and if he'd asked I would have said 'no'. I didn't want them here. I ran a comb through my wet hair and dressed in a hurry. No telling what they were up to.

The front door was wide open, and the first floor was stone cold. More laughter sounded from the front porch. Still barefoot, I snagged my leather jacket off the coat tree and went to see what was going on.

Two women, each with a smoldering smudge stick in their hand, smiled and posed while Lance snapped selfies of the three of them with his cell phone. The herbal scent of sage tickled my nose. The crescent scar on my palm itched.

Witches.

They were so focused on Lance, they didn't notice me. I recognized the dark-haired woman from the Shore Haven Public Library. The other, a willowy blonde I hadn't seen before, was making big time eyes at my brother.

"Hey, Lance," I said. "Watcha doin?"

"Keeping my promise, Matt." He nodded toward the blonde. "This is Robin Nygard. She's a warder—one of the best. She drove down from Toronto today, as a personal favor to me, to set up new wards of protection on the house. There is no ward that she crafts that can be undone." Lance slipped his arm around my waist and propelled me towards the witch. "This is my sister Mattie, who, in spite of all appearances to the contrary, is Madame Coumlie's direct descendant and Morta's Hand of Fate. She is the one person in the world I trust with both my life and my death."

The warmth of his words had me staring at Lance with new eyes. Since when had he gotten so smooth? So charming? Lance was full of surprises these days.

Robin nodded modestly. "I'm sorry for your loss, Mattie. I never knew your great grandmother, but I've heard many wonderful stories about her."

The dark-haired witch snorted. "When you asked us to renew the wards, I thought you meant for Henri.

You never said anything about *her*."

The venom in her voice caught me off guard.

"Now, Nettie," Lance began. "Don't be that way. Of course the wards are for Henri. It's his house. My sister is merely house-sitting for him."

"As if things weren't bad enough around here." Nettie tossed the still-burning smudge stick onto the snow-covered lawn. "People are dying; no thanks to you and your pet sorcerer."

"Hey, that's not fair," I protested. "Nobody wants John Fewkes stopped more than me. I did everything I could to stop it." It felt weird to be arguing with a witch about a renegade sorcerer.

"You're a bull in a china shop," Nettie sneered. "You have no idea how much damage you've caused. Now everyone believes that all the local witches are cultists—that we all answer to John Fewkes. It's only a matter of time before the government decides that witches are terrorists. That's a witch hunt that will make the Salem burnings look like a kiddie party. I hope they comes after you first, little Miss Finger of Fate. Serve you right."

She was stiff with fear. As much as I disliked the woman, I couldn't help but feel guilty. "We all want the same thing," I said. "The Feds don't want you, they want Fewkes stopped."

"Don't make excuses. Because of you, a lot of innocent people are being persecuted."

"No. Not because of me. John Fewkes released that demon. If you'll remember, I came to you for help—."

"I'm out of here." Nettie stomped down the walk to her car without another word and drove off.

Robin tossed her pale hair over her shoulder. "I'm sorry Lance. As a guest in their territory, Nettie insisted on coming today." she gave me a worried look. "Nettie may not be the easiest person to get on with, but she's right. The sisters are scared. They all believe that without the help of the Hand of Fate, the sorcerer could not have summoned the demon."

"They're wrong." I shook my head. "I tried to stop it—."

"Matt," Lance cut me off. "Let it go. You're never going to change the minds of Nettie and her coven. Robin isn't part of the local scene. You can trust her." They both gave me expectant looks. You can trust us both," he added, softly. "Tell us what happened."

Hoo boy.

Two cups of hot chocolate later and I'd told them just about everything that happened on Halloween night. The altars, the sacrifices, and even the part about Rhys being caught in the spirit tree. "I don't suppose you know how to get someone out of a spirit tree?"

"Sorry," Robin answered. "Not my area of expertise." Somehow, she'd managed to squeeze herself between Lance and me on the couch. "But I'd be glad to come back if you ever need something warded," she added, blushing. "Lance knows how to get hold of me."

After assuring both of us that the house was safely warded and that none but wanted visitors could gain entrance without explicit invitation from the resident, she left. Lance walked her to her car.

"She likes you," I told him, when he returned.

"It's more important to me that you're safe, Matt. I mean it."

At times like this, the years melted away and I was twelve again and he was my older, wiser, and so much cooler brother, who cared about me and kept me safe and made me do my homework and fed me and clothed me and made me feel loved. I wrapped my arms around his too-thin frame and hugged him. "Thank you, Lance. I mean it."

"How about giving me those tarot cards?"

"Geeze Laweeze, Lance." I shoved him away. "That's why you did this? So I'd give you the cards?" I snatched up the dirty cocoa cups and stomped into the kitchen. "You—no. Just no. Fricking. Way."

He trailed after me, unapologetic. "Come on, don't be that way. Admit it. You don't want them; you just don't want me to have them."

I set the dirty dishes in the sink and turned to face him. "Why do you want them?" In the other room, my cell phone began to ring. I ignored it. The cards belonged to me, dammit. They were the one thing of

Madame Coumlie's that she'd given to me. They were my legacy. Morta's symbol. She'd wanted me to have them.

Not Henri, not Rhys, and certainly not Lance.

CHAPTER 7

I DIDN'T CHECK my messages until I was on my way to work. Sheriff Reynolds wanted me to meet him at Hughie Green's office in the FBI building. He didn't say what it was, but his tone left me no doubt. "I want you here in ten minutes, Blackman."

Yeah, something was up. Since I was a potential witness in the Fewkes case, I had no role in the FBI manhunt. I wondered what made him change his mind.

When I arrived at the FBI field office on State Street, there was an undercurrent of excitement in the air. I was ushered into a large conference room on the third floor. The atmosphere was tense, as Agent Green and the Sheriff and several analysts intently examined aerial photographs spread across the center table. The walls were plastered with more photos, including several of Fewkes.

I paused, just inside the door, ill at ease. The tension in the room was palpable. I wasn't supposed to be here, let alone see this.

Agent Green noticed me first. "We just got a call from Fewkes. He's holding one of our agents hostage and claims you have something that belongs to him."

"What?" I looked to Sheriff Reynolds for a clue. "I don't—what are you talking about?"

"No bullshit, Deputy." Reynolds answered. "Fewkes says you've stolen his sister's book of spells. A grimoire." The amiable, easy-going good guy I thought I knew was gone. This was a bad-ass lawman on the hunt, and he'd leveled his attention right at me. Bad enough to make my stomach turn.

A vein throbbed at Green's temple. "He used my man's own cell phone to call us, knowing we'd trace the call. I don't negotiate with terrorists, but he's got my man, and I want that book. He says you had one of the werewolves steal it during the ritual."

I shook my head, appealing to both men. "I don't have it. If I did, I'd give it to you. Honest."

Kevin and the lycans had said something similar the other night. I thought back to the ritual. Had there been a book? It was possible. Liddy Fewkes must've had something to carry all her soul dolls in. A big bag. "Maybe one of the other cult members has it?"

I don't think so," Green said. "We got a tip from one of the cult members, saying that Fewkes has become unhinged about it. He's allegedly tortured very member of the coven, looking for it. He's got the cult in lockdown. No one is going in or out of the building."

"I swear I don't have it. Fewkes had already raised the summoning circle by the time I got there. We couldn't even get close to him. There was some kind of an impenetrable field surrounding them. I'm not a witch or a sorcerer—I couldn't get inside the circle. Then, when it did come down, that's when everything went south."

There's a soft knock at the door. An agent poked his head in, looking grave. "Missed him."

"And Cusick?" Green said.

He pressed his lips together and shook his head. "No dice. They've still got him."

The air went out of the room. Every face paled. Even Reynolds appeared sorely affected. Alma Waters was right; law enforcement was a brotherhood. A family.

The weight of their pain echoed within the hollowness of my own. I hadn't known the agent, but my failure to stop Fewkes from raising the Nalusa Falaya had made his life a living hell. His death would be on my hands. "How can I help?"

Ashen-faced, the sheriff passed me four mug shot photos. "We've interviewed all the local alphas. No one is talking. Give us the names of the lycans who were at the ritual."

The realization that every alpha in the county had a mug shot tore through me like an arrow through the heart. I knew none of them personally—Kevin had been the only lycan I'd known at the time. Giving them his name wouldn't get them what they wanted, but it would get them Kevin's name and picture to add to their rogues gallery. Kevin didn't have the book. "I'm sorry, I can't"

"Can't or won't," barked Green.

"Come on, Mattie," Reynolds said. "I know you know something. Give."

"We put out a call for volunteers. I never saw any of them in human form and no one was exactly wearing nametags. None of them came near the circle. They were only meant to be a distraction."

"So *you* say," Green said.

"I mean it. The local lycans refused to participate. They knew that the cultists had been stalking them and would immediately recognize them in wolf form, so they stayed away. You can ask your snitch inside the cult to confirm it." I made a mental note to get to know and recognize all the lycans in the area, starting with Monroe County.

"Easy Mattie," Reynolds cautioned. "Cusick, the agent who was kidnapped, is the inside man."

The room had gone eerily quiet.

The sour tang of acid burned the back of my throat. "I'm sorry," I choked.

"We've got to find that book," Green said.

Reynolds rubbed his chin. "Lou was my go-to guy on lycan stuff, but now it's you, rookie. Talk to them. Find out who's got it. We've got to get our hands on it before Fewkes does. Whatever he wants, we can't let him have it."

"I'm on it," I said. I remembered the white wolf. Surely Kevin must've known him. "Give me a few days."

"We don't have a few days," Green said. "People are dying."

"Just to be clear, Mattie, we aren't asking you to *do* anything," Reynolds cautioned. "Just get us the names of the lycans who were at the ritual. We'll take it from there."

No can do. "Yes sir." I couldn't just turn over a list of names. Whoever had the book might not even know what it was. If I brought them the book, it wouldn't matter who had it.

Dismissed, I paused at the door. "He's got an immortal demon at his beck and call," I said. "How are you going to stop him?"

"You leave that to us, Deputy," Green answered. "Find that book and we'll take it from there."

CHAPTER 8

IT WAS ALMOST midnight by the time I hit the street—of course I headed straight for Growlers Pub. Some parts of Halloween night were clear to me—others, not so much. I had only hazy memories of what was going on inside the ritual circle before the wards around the summoning circle came down. Was there a book there? I'd been too busy watching Fewkes—I hadn't paid that much attention to what Liddy was doing or whether or not she had a book.

At the stoplight, I turned up the heat in the Subaru. It didn't seem to be working right—the car was still as cold as it had been in the garage.

A flicker of movement from the passenger seat was the only warning I had before John Fewkes materialized in the passenger seat. Before I could react, he'd grabbed me by the throat.

"You stupid bitch," he hissed. His fingers dug into

my neck.

I clawed at him—I tried to squirm away, but the seat belt hampered my movements.

John Fewkes's appearance had altered dramatically since I'd seen him last. The great walrus moustache was still there, but the banker's physique and posh clothing were gone—as was his lifeline. Immortality had changed Fewkes. It was as if all the weakness in him had been stripped away. His body felt hard and lean—his clothes hung loose on his now wiry frame. "You think wards can keep you safe from me? Do you have any idea what you've—?"

I tromped the gas pedal to the metal and the car shot forward. Like a scene out of *Bullitt*, the Subaru burned rubber and whipped left, crossing two lanes of oncoming traffic. We caromed off a parked car, and bounced over the curb into a strip mall parking lot, before plowing onto the front window of the See Spot Go Dry Cleaners. In a shatter of glass, the airbags deployed. Without a seatbelt, Fewkes rebounded off his airbag, right into the windshield.

Freed from his grip, I gave silent thanks to the Subaru gods and unfastened my seatbelt. I managed to get the door open, but dazed and bloody as he was; Fewkes grabbed me by my hair before I could get out of the car.

"He tricked me, you twit!" Fewkes held onto me with all the desperation of a drowning man. "That devil and I are linked now. The FBI knows who I am. They blame me for the killings. This is all *your* fault!" His sour breath washed over me.

I fought to get him off me, but could not escape his grasp. We tumbled out of the car onto the frozen pavement. Fewkes lay on top of me, using his weight to hold me down. Broken glass crunched beneath my leather jacket. From inside the shop, an alarm went off. Someone would be coming. *Keep him talking.* "How is this my fault," I panted. "You're the one who summoned him."

"If not for you I'd be in Monte Carlo or Macao by now--instead of this frozen hell. I can't leave!"

His spittle splashed hot against my cheek. "What are you talking about," I gasped. The smell of smoke clung to him. "You're his master, *he has to obey you!*"

"That's the problem, you imbecile—I'm not his master. He's more powerful than me, He's more powerful than you can imagine."

I gritted my teeth. "Well, well. Karma *is* a bitch, ain't it?"

He punched me in the diaphragm.

I curled into a fetal position and gasped for breath, fighting not to lose consciousness.

"I was never going to actually release him. If you hadn't have interfered, I wouldn't have collapsed—and he could never have escaped. The longer he's free, the more powerful he becomes. He is obsessed with the

Muse. He wants her back. Get up."

My arms and legs were not cooperating.

He hauled me to my feet and shook me like a ragdoll until my teeth rattled. "You killed my sister. You've ruined my life. Give me back that spell book, or I'll be tied to him for eternity."

"I don't have it." I gasped.

He shoved his hand up my shirt, pressing his hard, bony fingers to my chest. A wave of lethargy passed over me, leaving only a dull ache in my back and gut. My heart skipped a beat.

And another.

And another. My heart lubbed weakly. My arms and legs felt dead already.

"Give. It. To. Me. Bitch." With every word, my vision grew darker.

"I swear, I don't know where it is!" My back clenched in a sudden spasm. "Stop it--." I groaned. "Please." I grunted. Blackness closed in—my voice sounded like it was coming from a million miles away. Colored lights danced at the edge of my vision. I felt like I was being sucked down a long tunnel. "Why do you need it?"

"Give it to me and I will let you live."

A cold sense of dread surged through me. I swear my heart stopped beating. "No, wait. I think—I think I can find it. Gimme a f-few days."

He took his hand off my heart and grabbed a fistful

of my hair. "The tree saps his strength. It keeps him weak. If I don't get him back into the tree soon, it'll be too late. The clock is ticking."

I gasped with relief, even as the back spasm continued to drain my resistance. "You can open the tree?"

"Yes." He hissed. "And that means I'm also the only one who get your boyfriend back."

Rhys. The thought of him struck me like a physical blow. The anger cleared my head.

"But I need that book of spells to do it. Tick-tock, little girl. Time is wasting. Do this, and we can fix everything while the FBI is still running around with their panties on fire. I can see through its eyes, you know. For some reason, it thinks you're different from other mortals."

He must've seen something in my face. With a final shake, he shoved me away from him. "I am the only chance you have to stop him. Get me that book."

I gritted my teeth against the spasm, even as it began to subside. There was no reason for Fewkes to lie about the spell book. It must've been Liddy who worked the spell to open the tree the first time. It made sense that he'd need the grimoire to do it now. This might be the only way to free Rhys. In the distance a siren howled. I didn't have much time.

I gave a single nod. "Okay." I grunted through the pain. "How do I get in touch with you?"

But he was already gone, leaving only a smoky stench behind.

By the time the tow truck dropped me off at the parking garage beneath the Sheriff's station, it was nearly time for the morning shift to arrive. My hands shook as I dialed Kevin's cell phone number. No one answered. I sat in the parking garage in my Honda, with the heater on full blast, wondering when Fewkes might decide to show up next. I didn't think I'd survive a second encounter. I wondered if cars could be protected with wards. I was never going to live down crashing my patrol vehicle into the front window of the See Spot Go Dry Cleaners.

The sound of a car door slam woke me up. A glance at Rusty's clock told me I'd been asleep for twenty minutes. I tried Kevin's number again, with no better luck.

Sheriff Reynolds was an early bird. I dreaded the lecture, but it would be better if he heard about the Subaru from me first. Better to face him now than later. I turned off the car and gingerly made my way upstairs to his office.

I caught him in the break room as he was pouring

his first cup of coffee of the day. Even at that hour, he'd already heard the news. "Seriously? Black ice?"

That was the story I'd written up. The story I'd told the first responders. The story I'd tell anyone who asked. But Jim Reynolds wasn't just anyone. He was the guy who had given me my dream gig. He'd taken my oath. And now, in this grey light of this winter morning, I couldn't go through with it.

He must've sensed my indecision. "Come on," he jerked his head toward his office.

With the door closed, I managed to tell him the most of it. How John Fewkes had showed up and how in trying to keep him from strangling me, I'd used the car as a weapon.

"Obviously, it didn't work," I confessed. "But I found out why he wants the book. He says something went wrong during the ritual. He's tied to the demon, now, not the other way around. He believes that the spell his sister used to summon it can also be used stop it." No point in telling him about Rhys. I paused. "I am sorry about the Subaru."

"Green knows you lied to him in the hospital, but wasn't sure about what. He thought you might be tied to the cult. He's had an agent tailing you from the beginning. He saw the whole thing go down." The ghost of a smile flashed across his face. "Don't worry about the car. Given your reputation, I'm surprised it took this long."

My cheeks grew warm. Rather than feeling relieved, the knot in my stomach clenched a little tighter. This had been a test. To find out if I'd tell him the truth. "Do you think I'm in on this with Fewkes? Everybody else seems to think so. Is that why you offered me the job?"

His chin jutted forward as he considered his words. "You're a wild card, Deputy. The job was, and still is, legit. Moreover, I think you've got as good a chance as anyone of finding that book, so get on it. The bodies are piling up. "

Tick-tock. "Yes sir."

CHAPTER 9

I DROVE STRAIGHT home and fell asleep lying across my bed, fully clothed. Two hours later, I woke up gasping for breath, after dreaming that Fewkes had stopped my heart, just as I was about to pull Rhys from the spirit tree. I lay in bed, feeling reassured by the insistent pounding of my heart: *tick-TOCK, tick-TOCK*.

Time to go.

I tried Kevin's phone again, but still no answer. Growlers would be open for lunch soon. Might as well head out there. After a quick shower and change of clothes, I tripped downstairs and headed toward the kitchen to grab a strawberry Pop-Tart for the road.

Lance was seated at the kitchen table with his shirt off, doctoring the infected imbed. His djemon, Jinxey, perched comfortably on his bare shoulder, watching Lance's every movement with bright interest. The infection around his implant had spread; long, streaks of red reached for his heart.

Just the thing to put a girl off her Pop-Tart.

"That thing is getting worse, not better," I told him. "You look awful, Lance."

"Shut up, it's nothing." He shot me an irritated glance and then did a double-take. "What happened to you?"

Self consciously, I reached for my neck. The angry purple marks left by Fewkes' fingers had already faded to yellow. They'd be gone completely in a few hours. "Shut up, it's nothing."

For a beat, we were brother and sister again, instead of two broken secrets.

"Truth tell, Lance," I said, invoking the game we made up as kids. While she was alive, our mother never spoke a single word of truth in her life—at least not to the police, or the neighbors, or the people from Child Protective Services. And never, *ever* to us. Truth Tell was for things too horrible to say out loud, but which could not be contained. Things like, *my mother is a whore*; or *I am a bastard.* "What is that thing you've got embedded in your chest? Tell me true."

He slumped back in his chair. "It's a relic. A sliver from Fortune's Wheel—the Rota Fortunae. The original wheel from the goddess Fortuna's chariot."

I gave him a hard stare. He wasn't kidding. "You stole it?"

He shook his head. "Of course not. Abe got it for me." He nodded as I recognized the name. "That's right, the same old man who brought you Fate's shears. Yeah, I know all about them. Truth told, Matt. Now give me that tarot deck and I'll be out of your hair."

I'd met Abe Lightner during the Spirit Festival. He's a traveler of sorts, able to cross the veils between the living and the dead as easily as Charlie does. An old friend of Madame Coumlie's, she'd asked him to be on the lookout for Fate's shears in his travels. She died before he found them. As her heir, Abe had given them to me.

Why would Lance ask Abe to get him a sliver of Fortune's wheel?

Because he thought it would bring him luck.

Of course. Lance had always been superstitious. He'd been one of Madame Coumlie's regular clients for years. Unlike me, Lance believed in all that fortune teller stuff. We have different fathers, but we are both descended of Morta's line. That didn't explain why Abe would give Lance the relic of a goddess. The imbed on Lance's chest took on a new significance.

Truth told, but it didn't make sense. "Just tell me why the cards are so important to you."

"Because I need them—Isn't that enough? Why do you always do this, Matt? Because I'm your brother. Because I practically raised you. Because I'm asking you."

Without warning, Blix appeared, sitting atop kitchen table, his coal-black feathers fluffed agog.

"I have found the Muse," he announced.

CHAPTER 10

"WHAT IS HE talking about," Lance asked.

I waved off his question. "What? Where? Tell me, Blix!"

Evidently pleased by my reaction to his news, Blix shook out his wing feathers and smoothed them into place. "In the Penfield family vault."

I remembered how the Nalusa Falaya had curled up on the roof of the marble tomb. "You're saying the crypt is the *muse*? I don't get it."

"No, Mistress. The name on the crypt is E. M. Penfield. Evelyn Muse Penfield was the first wife of Edmond Penfield, the first European settler in the region." Blix wrapped his tail around his feet, looking rather smug.

Ugh. I hated him to call me Mistress. Apparently, demon protocol demanded it. "And you're saying she's the Muse?"

"I believe that Evelyn Penfield may have been the first of the Penfield witches. She was seventeen, and newly married when she and Edmond arrived in the area. The historical society in Rush has an extensive archive of the Penfield family, including two of Evelyn's diaries. Based on the entries I found, Evelyn felt isolated here and missed her family terribly. She spent much of her time with the local Senequois tribeswomen, teaching them English in exchange for learning local herb lore. Having come all the way from England, the Penfields were unfamiliar with the brutal winters of northern New York. They were probably the first to seek out the expertise of the indigenous locals.

"Evelyn became very close to one of the Senequois women, Inuk-ya, a shaman in the local tribe, and her young daughter, whose true name is unknown. Inuk-ya taught the Penfields how and when to plant their crops, and what forage was best for their livestock. Through her tutelage and friendship, the Penfields fared far better than their neighbors. Eventually, other women in the area sought out the wisdom of the Senequois mystics.

"Three years after the Penfields settled in the area, a smallpox epidemic struck. Many Senequois tribal members died, including Inuk-ya. Devastated by the loss of her friend, Evelyn brought the medicine woman's 11-year-old daughter to live with her as a sister. In spite of his doubts, she managed to persuade her husband Edmond to accept the girl into his household.

"This caused great upset in the tribe. The elders complained to Edmond, saying the girl belonged with her own people. She was born with her mother's gift—she would be expected to take her instructions in preparation for taking over Inuk-ya's role in the tribe.

"Evelyn would not stand to think of a lovely young girl being forced into such a hard life—not when she had no children to care for, and was alone all day while Edmond tended the fields. The elders eventually relented, saying that the girl could spend part of her time in the white man's world, but was still obligated to her important role as a shaman for the tribe.

"The girl's adoption caused consternation among the other settlers as well, but everyone could see how Evelyn doted on the child—she even cut up her own dresses and altered them to fit the girl. Evelyn taught her to read and write, and the child was polite and well-spoken. When Evelyn brought the girl to church, it was discovered that she had an astonishingly beautiful singing voice. So lovely, in fact that people called her Evelyn's Muse, or simply, the Muse."

This was, by far, the longest speech I'd ever heard from Blix. "And you're saying that this Senequois girl is the Muse that the Nalusa Falaya was asking me about."

"Don't tell me you've been talking to that smoke

devil," Lance said, incredulous. "Are you nuts?"

"It's not a devil. It's an elemental demon of the Senequois people," I answered. "Go on, Blix."

"Yeah, like that makes a difference," muttered Lance.

"The girl lived with the Penfields for three years, until Evelyn's death. Edmond, who by all reports grieved his wife's passing deeply, commissioned the marble crypt in the family cemetery in memory of his wife. The Muse, who was fourteen at the time, was also deeply affected, and suffered from extreme bouts of melancholy—unable or unwilling to sing in church. She also refused her obligations to the elders of the Senequois tribe. The other women of the settlement observed that she straddled two worlds now, and no longer felt part of either. Under Edmond's discipline, the Muse became increasingly rebellious and spent more and more time at Evelyn's tomb.

"When his daughter did not present herself for church one Sunday, Edmond went out to the cemetery to get her and discovered her body inside his wife's burial vault. The newspaper of the time said she died of a broken heart, although there was some speculation that she may have taken her own life. In her obituary, she is referred to as Muse Penfield."

Blix gazed at me expectantly.

"That's it?"

His ears drooped. "You asked me to find out

everything I could about the Muse." After a pause, he added, "I await your command."

I bit back my frustration. Words and phrasing are extremely important to djemons. I didn't remember exactly what terms I'd used when I asked Blix to find out who the Muse was, but I had no doubt he'd done precisely as I'd asked—no more, no less. It was impossible for him to do otherwise.

"Did her obituary happen to mention where she was buried?"

His ears drooped further. "No, Mistress. There are several family portraits, personal effects and family items that were donated to the Historical Society. Your powers as Morta's Hand have grown stronger. Perhaps, if you were to handle them, you may be able to discern more about the Muse."

Dang. While Blix could get into Fort Knox in the blink of an eye, breaking into the Rush Historical Society to grope some old books was not something I could explain if I got caught.

"Were you able to discover a connection between the Nalusa Falaya and the Muse?"

Blix slumped miserably. "No, Mistress."

This was going nowhere, and while I knew better than to coddle him, I would not willingly make him feel bad when he obeyed my command. "Thank you, Blix. That will be all."

He departed the visible plane without comment,

although I knew he was probably curled up in his usual spot on top of the bookcase in the parlor. Out of sight, if not out of hearing.

I stood for a moment, hands on my hips, trying to decide what to do next. According to Charlie, the Nalusa Falaya was some sort of Senequois bogeyman—their version of Freddy Kruger. Maybe wanting the Muse meant something. Maybe it liked little girls. Yuck. Or maybe it meant nothing.

Tick-tock.

Whatever it meant, I was running out of time. Nothing Blix had discovered about the Muse altered the fact that I had to get my hands on Liddy Fewkes' book of spells. Without it, more people would die, including Rhys.

"Talk to me, Matt," Lance said. "Tell me what's going on."

I'd forgotten he was there. He still hadn't told me why he wanted those damn Tarot cards so much, but I didn't have time to ask about it now.

"Later," I said. I was already on the move. I grabbed my jacket off the hall tree and shrugged myself into it, checking the pockets to make sure I had Henri's gloves with me. "I've gotta see a man about a wolf."

Tick tock.

CHAPTER 11

I SPED UP Route 104, on my way to Growlers Pub. As I crossed the bridge, I noticed that the bay which separated Shore Haven from Webster had frozen solid. Winter had settled in for the duration.

I was stopped for a red light at the intersection at Five Mile and Plank Road, when two unmarked black Chevy Tahoe SUVs sped right past me at good clip. My first thought was that they had to be Feds—my second that they had to be on a call. Only one thing would get the FBI racing through red lights in Penfield.

Another victim.

I hit the gas and took off after them. Fortunately, traffic was light, and I didn't have far to go. Both cars pulled into the parking lot of Knutt's Apple Farm, where they joined a half-dozen other vehicles with tinted windows and the county coroner's black van.

I spotted FBI agent-in-charge Hughie Green

and Sheriff Reynolds speaking to Craig Farrens, the coroner. My phone vibrated as I got out of the car, but I ignored it, zipping up my jacket and strolling over like I belonged there. Reynolds saw me and waved me over.

"That was quick," he said. "I just left you a message."

"I was in the neighborhood. What's up?"

"We're just about finished up here. Two new victims—er, one and change. An agent and a big alpha lycan. It's pretty gruesome. The agent and his partner had the alpha under surveillance. They followed him here."

"Knutt's is closed for the season," I said.

"No shit. The Feds thought the lycan might be up to something, but it looks like they got caught up in an ambush instead. By the time they got close enough to see the action, it was too late. The surviving agent says a thirty-foot tall man of smoke came out of the trees and attacked the lycan. The alpha shifted into wolf form, but that didn't help. When he tried to shift back to human form, the smoke guy--."

"The Nalusa Falaya," I corrected him. "The immortal creature John Fewkes summoned. It's not a guy, or a man, or even an ordinary demon."

"Right." Reynolds gave me a *whatever* shrug. "Anyway, according to the witness, the ah, Falaya thing picked him up and bit him in half. All that's left is the bottom half."

Hughie Green walked up beside us. "Agent Wong emptied his gun into the creature," he said. "Bullets passed right through it, with no effect. Then it killed the agent with a single blow and just evaporated. Tell me something, Blackman. Why is it that every time somebody dies in this town, you show up?" Hughie Green bristled with barely contained anger. "This is the second agent I've lost in as many days. What are you doing here, Deputy?"

Reynolds jumped in before I could answer. "She's here to identify the lycan."

"Where's his car," I asked, hoping I knew the owner. Most of the cars in the lot looked like they belonged to the Feds.

"Forget it," Green smirked. "We already know who it is. Where's the book, Blackman? It's our only link to the demon's master."

"I'm working on it. But you're wrong about Fewkes; he's not the Nalusa Falaya's master."

"Thank you, Deputy Smartass," Green retorted. "But as it happens, I know a thing or two about demon masters. The guy that summons the demon is the master. That's the way it works."

"Look, I know your men saw Fewkes came after me." I glanced at Reynolds, who nodded. "You know he wants the book, but you don't know why. Well, he told me why. It's because he--." *Oh crap.* I couldn't tell

Green about the spirit tree—they might try to burn it or chop it down.

"What? What does he want?" Green looked like he was about to explode.

"Fewkes says the demon is in charge. He says it's stronger than he is—it has the power to keep him from leaving. He needs the spell book to, um—to send it back where it came from."

Green pressed his lips together and shook his head. "I don't believe you. If Fewkes isn't controlling the thing, who is?"

"That's what I'm trying to tell you," I answered. "This is no ordinary demon. It answers to no one. Fewkes believes he needs the book to control it."

"So where's the book?" Reynolds asked.

"I don't know," I answered.

"You know where it is, though," accused Green.

"Not yet," I answered. "But I'm working on it."

"Well then get out of here and get me that book!"

CHAPTER 12

News of the murder had already reached the pub. Nash Redleaf had been the beloved alpha of the Penfield pack. The place was eerily silent.

I'd met Alpha Redleaf twice—enough to recognize him, but not well enough to call him friend. He had the oddly oversized neck and musculature of an alpha, paired with enough charisma that he never had to use his strength to win an argument. His death would affect every werewolf in the county. A memorial had already been set up at Redleaf's permanently reserved booth in the back of the bar—stones, an evergreen bough, a bit of broken antler, feathers, even prayer beads. Redleaf had been proud of his native roots.

No one spoke. Lycan and human patrons alike slumped over their beers in small groups. Growlers was the pack's clubhouse. Every single person in the place clearly and deeply mourned his loss. Several of the women and one or two of the men, wept openly. Bad enough that the lycans felt persecuted by the Witches. With a sense of growing unease, an undercurrent of impending violence sent a shiver through me.

As upset as he was, Kevin immediately agreed to speak to me outside.

"I just heard about it," I said. "I'm so sorry for your loss."

"You have no idea what it's like." Kevin's eyes were red-rimmed. "Losing Nash is like losing a parent. Or a child. Or a leg." He wiped his face on his sleeve. "He made us strong. He kept us safe."

"Look, I know this is a bad time, but I need to know if any of the werewolves at the ritual took anything."

Kevin raised his eyes to mine, but his eyes were focused inward. "A pack is connection. Through the minds and hearts of many, we are one. One arrow can easily be broken, but when arrows are bound together, they become strong. He was the arrow we bound ourselves to."

I gripped his hand, willing him to listen to me. "I hear what you're saying. I'm trying to stop this and I need you to pay attention. Help me stop Nash's killer before anyone else has to die."

With visible effort he came back to himself. He nodded. "Okay."

"Liddy's spell book went missing that night. I need to find it."

His eyes grew distant with the memory. I thought I'd lost him again.

He sighed. "You were there, same as me. Everyone stayed in the woods until the signal. No one got close enough to take anything from her. Only me and Silas, and I swear, I didn't take anything."

"At one point, I know some of the wolves came out of the woods. Maybe someone found it." I glanced at the door to the bar. "Maybe we could ask the folks inside..."

"No, Mattie. I was the only one from Penfield. The others were from Silas's pack."

I remembered the white wolf. "Okay, how do I get hold of Silas? This is important. I've got to get that book."

Kevin eyes widened in understanding. "He's going to murder everyone in the pack, isn't he?"

"No one knows for sure what he's going to do next. All I know is that I've got to find that book. I need to talk to Silas."

He nodded. "Alright. I'll set it up."

CHAPTER 13

THE EGG HEAVEN café was jammed—the aroma of homemade bread, bacon, and fresh-brewed coffee told me this place lived up to its name. The joint was located in a quaint little village on the shore of Canandaigua Lake, situated in the heart of the Finger Lakes region.

I scanned the room, not knowing who I was looking for. At least a third of the customers appeared to be lycan. Most people thought that a thick neck was the tell-tale of a person affected with lycanthropy, but for me, their lifeline was unmistakable—a twisted, double thread of two different colors that glowed unnaturally bright. In human form, one color predominated, in wolf form; it was the other, so recognizing the human that belonged to a particular wolf I'd only met once was impossible.

From a back booth, a big guy with skin the color of

espresso waved me over.

I grinned and made my way toward him. So this was the big white wolf. Somehow, the memory of the man's beast fit perfectly with the guy sitting before me. There was something familiar about his open, half-amused expression; or maybe it was something in his eyes—I felt an immediate connection to him.

"Silas?" I asked.

"Yeah," he replied, scooting over in the booth to make room for me. "Have a seat, Mattie. This is Mike."

I slipped into the warm vinyl booth next to Silas and got a good look at the dark-haired guy sitting across from him. Lean, athletic and clean cut, Mike's stony expression gave away nothing.

He wasn't human, but he wasn't lycan or dhampir or anything else I'd encountered before. His lifeline pulsed with every hue and color of the rainbow, and then some. Alive, but—whatever he was, I had no clue. And yet, there was something unmistakably familiar about him.

"You're a cop," I said.

"Used to be," he answered with a mildness at odds with his feral aura.

"He's pack, Mattie," Silas said, as if to forestall any further questions. "Kevin said you wanted to talk to me. What's up?"

"I'm looking for something. A book. It disappeared the night of the ritual. Lost or maybe picked up by someone who was there."

"What kind of book," Mike asked, around a mouthful of steak and eggs.

"Just a book. It belonged to Liddy Fewkes. The Feds are looking for it, too."

Silas glanced at Mike before answering. "Why do you want it?"

"Do you have it?"

Silas shook his head. "Sorry, no."

I slumped back in my seat. I'd been so certain that I was on the right track. Without that book— *oh Rhys.* A sudden lump in my throat forced me to blink back tears.

"This have anything to do with Redleaf's murder?" Mike asked.

I sighed. "It's complicated."

Silas slid his half-full cup of coffee toward me, one eyebrow cocked.

I drained in a long swallow. "You guys were my only hope."

"Guess you made the trip for nothing," Silas answered. He motioned to the waitress for more coffee.

I wasn't buying it.

These guys knew more than they were saying. I could feel it. Maybe I'd picked up a thing or two from the Penfield pack. There was a subtle tension at the table that hadn't been there when I sat down. Lycans are naturally wary of anyone outside the pack. Kevin might have vouched for me, but that wouldn't be enough to sway these two. There was something else going on here, too. Their body language was all wrong for two pack pals having breakfast together.

The waitress brought over another cup for me and poured fresh coffee all around. Mike took his coffee black, but Silas took his with cream, like me.

If wolf patrol had taught me anything, it was that lycans had an uncanny way of sniffing out a lie. I'd been going about this all wrong. I slurped my coffee, and made a conscious effort to release the tension in my shoulder. Mmmm. The coffee was delicious. I was among friends here, I told myself. I had nothing to hide from either of these men.

"It's a book of spells," I began. "John Fewkes is desperate to get it back. He says he needs it to free himself from the demon's control. He says the ritual his sister used to summon the Nalusa Falaya can also be used to put it back into the spirit tree. The FBI thinks he wants it to make himself more powerful. They want to get it before he does."

"You haven't answered the question," Mike said. "Why do *you* want the book?"

"I was there, Mattie." Silas took a sip of coffee. "I saw what happened. Word is, Rhys Warrick is pack to you."

I nodded, biting my lips together to stifle the stab of pain in my heart. *Pack to you.* Three little words, but they said so much. Far more than *boyfriend* could ever mean. Damn, these guys were good.

"Yes," I hissed. "*He is pack to me.*" I pulled a crumpled tissue out of my pocket and blew my nose, furious at my own weakness. "He's still alive in that damn sprit tree. Look, the Nalusa Falaya controls Fewkes right now—the sorcerer is his virtual prisoner. Fewkes must put the Nalusa Falaya back into the tree if he wants his life back. Trapped inside the spirit tree, the Nalusa Falaya will be too weak to control him, but he will retain his shared immortality with the demon. That spell book is the only way to break its hold over him. And when Fewkes opens the tree, it'll be the only chance I have to get Rhys out of there."

"The sorcerer is a liar," Mike said. "You know he's playing you."

"For what purpose? I can't hurt him, he's immortal now." I paused. "Okay, maybe he is," I admitted. "But they used the spell book to open the tree the first time. Like it or not, he's the only person alive who has the power to open that tree a second time."

Neither man spoke, but something passed between them—almost like an unspoken conversation. I felt a curious current of energy pass between them; like the little door in my head that Morta used to speak to me. I stole another glance at Mike. *Who was this guy?*

Silas broke the silence. "I did find a book, but it's not the one you're looking for. What I found was an old hymnal. Very old. There were pages covered in writing," He rushed to explain. "No spells. It was written in a child's hand. You know, like the kind of writing kids do to practice their letters. Or a diary. Juvenile stuff."

A jolt of adrenaline rushed through me.

"No spells whatsoever," Mike cautioned.

"How would you know?" I asked.

"I was there when he found it," Mike answered. "Believe me, I'd know." Something moved behind his eyes as he said it. Whatever he was, I believed him. At the same time, I had to see it for myself.

"Where is it now?"

Silas pushed his empty plate away. "I found it lying on the grass on the way in. It smelled like the Liddy witch. I didn't know what to do with it, but I didn't want to leave it there. I put it in the big crypt at the rendezvous spot." He shrugged. "As far as I know, it's still there."

I tried to remember if I'd seen a book lying around when Blix and I had been holed up inside. "I was in there after the ritual. I didn't see a book."

"Of course not," Silas grinned. An utterly wolfish expression crossed his features. "Like any good wolf, I buried it. South corner. About six inches down."

CHAPTER 14

BY THE TIME I left Egg Heaven, it was far too cold and dark to go poking around in the cemetery at night without warmer clothes. I had a pair of down coveralls and thermal underwear at the house that would keep me warm enough. And I'd need a shovel. I had a feeling that in spite of what the guys had told me, that hymn book held the answers I was looking for.

Lance met me at the front door. "You're home early."

"I just came home to change--." I froze, suddenly speechless.

My Victory Hammer S motorcycle, currently owned by Lance's former business partner, Doc, was sitting in the middle of the entryway.

The alluring scent of leather polish and chrome polish tickled my nose. I couldn't help myself. I ran my hand across the gleaming handlebars. "What have you done, Lance?"

"Pink slip is on the kitchen table," he said. "She's all yours," he added, with a wry smile. "Again."

"Where'd you get the money?"

He wiped a sheen of sweat off his forehead. His eyes were bright with fatigue. And more than a little pride. "You want it or not?"

"Yes! Yes, of course. I just want to know why--." I stopped. I already knew the answer.

As if he'd heard my thoughts, my brother gave me a slow nod. "Give me the cards, Matt."

The Vic's leather seat was doeskin soft. I couldn't say no to him. Not this time. He knew it, too. "Just tell me why you want them."

"Bad luck, Sis." He picked up a half-empty pint of Rye whiskey and took a swig. "Isn't it enough that I'm your brother? I need them and you don't. Is that what you want to hear?"

The answer hit me and he didn't have to say it. I held onto the Vic for support. "You're dying."

He snorted. "Madame Coumlie was never wrong. Not once. She could always tell me what I needed to do to change my luck. It wasn't until you told me that she was our great-grandmother, that it hit me. I've got her blood in my veins, too. Not as much as you, but its there."

"Oh Lance, I'm sorry."

"Lord Luck, she called me, and she was right. Luck

has always ruled my life. Only I've been on a real bad streak lately, and unless I can come out of it, I'm going down." He put his hand to his chest. "This sliver of wood embedded beneath my skin is the only thing keeping me alive right now."

I shook my head in disbelief. "It's just superstition, Lance. Those cards can't heal you."

"Listen to me, Matt. Luck is a cycle. A wheel. Like, karma, right? What goes around comes around. The cards tell me how to change my luck groove when things are on the downswing."

"Oh come on—you can't possibly believe that crap."

"It's not crap. The cards aren't magic, they're a tool. You and I are descended from the greatest oracle the world has ever known. Old lady Coumlie was a watered down version, but she still had the juice. I figure I've got enough of her in me so that I can tap into that. Now give me those cards."

My brother was dying. I would not say no to him again. "Wait here," I told him.

I opened the secret compartment behind the built-in bookcase in the parlor. Blindly, I reached inside and pulled out the deck of domino-sized tiles, wrapped in an orange scarf.

Lance seemed to perk up at the sight of the scarf-wrapped bundle in my hand.

I hesitated. "They're extremely fragile."

"I don't want to break them. I just want to use them."

I didn't feel right about it, but in spite of everything, Lance and I were pack, too. Like the lycans, said, he was *forever pack* to me, as I was to him. No matter what either of us did or said in the past or the future, that would never change. If he were in my place, *he would do the same for me.*

I handed over the orange bundle of my inheritance. "Do what you have to do, Lance. I can't stay." I ran upstairs and changed into my cold-weather gear, adding a wool scarf and my sheepskin-lined trapper hat. I clumped downstairs and paused at the front door. "Thanks for the Vic, Lance," I yelled.

There was no answer. But then, I hadn't expected one, either.

CHAPTER 15

DRESSED WARMLY, WITH a shovel from Madame Coumlie's garage and a spare set of batteries for the flashlight, I drove toward Knutt's Apple Farm. In spite of my determination to retrieve the book from the Evelyn Penfield's crypt, Lance held my thoughts. My brother wouldn't tell me his exact diagnosis, but it didn't matter. We both knew in our guts that it wasn't the kind of thing that would respond to modern medicine.

I parked the car in the empty lot and trudged through the crisp snow. Frigid conditions, but this time, I was dressed for it. Much of the snow on the trail leading through the leafless orchard had evaporated, and the going was better than I expected. With Blix on one shoulder, and a shovel on the other, I was positive that the book Silas had buried was the one I was looking for.

"What will you do if the Nalusa Falaya is there?" asked Blix. "Or the sorcerer?"

I stumbled, nearly taking a header into the snow. "That would be awkward," I admitted. The shovel would be a bit sticky to explain. I paused at the top of the vale to catch my breath and flashed the light across the tomb below us, looking for any sign of Fewkes or the Nalusa Falaya. I didn't see anything, but that didn't mean they weren't there.

"You see anything?" I asked.

"Perhaps they are inside."

I considered the possibility. "I don't think so. I don't think either of them can enter the vault. Maybe it's holy ground or something." I started down the trail. "I think that if they were here, they would have shown themselves by now. We haven't exactly been quiet."

"Perhaps the vault is warded," suggested Blix.

"Maybe," I agreed. I followed the trail, using the shovel to break up icy patches in the snow, until we reached the entrance to Evelyn Penfield's crypt. I flashed the light around inside the vault. Blix scampered over to the south corner, an unpaved area on the very back wall. "The soil here looks to have been disturbed," he said.

Blix was right. Wolf tracks across the marble floor backed up Silas's story. I gave Blix the flashlight and started digging. The book was right where Silas said it would be. I found it almost immediately, buried just beneath the third shovelful.

It was much smaller than I expected—about the size of my open palm, wrapped in a square of dark brown, embossed leather. When I unwrapped it, I knew with certainty that I'd found what I was looking for. I checked the title page and grinned at the hand-written inscription. Part of the name had been scratched out, but was still legible:

Property of ~~Evelyn~~ Muse ~~Penfield.~~

I riffled through the pages, many of them worn and stained. Silas was right. This was no spell book— it was a hymnal. Page after page of religious music and text. Additional sheets of loose paper, yellowed with age, had been slipped into the back of the book and seemed to be diary entries. One in particular, caught my eye.

"He watches me from the deep shade of the woods, thinking I don't see, but I know he is there, watching me. He comes every day. Yesterday, when my keening turned to song, he showed himself to me. Please don't stop, he told me, when he stepped out of the trees. Your song, your voice—so beautiful. It haunts me... Please, don't be afraid—."

A frigid wave of cold air washed over me. I skimmed through more pages.

"...cleave unto only him because we love each other... Father is becoming suspicious...found my diary...accused me of meeting one of the men of my

clan...I would never...only him..."

The chill inside the crypt turned even colder, distracting me from the page. I felt a presence. Blix pricked up his ears—he felt it, too.

"Turn off the light, Blix," I said.

In the sudden darkness, I could see her hazy outline, hovering near the ceiling above us. She was petite, with long flowing hair, dressed in a simple smock and apron. Her feet were bare.

My first ghost. Charlie was right about my growing powers.

"It's *mine*," she hissed, her words a bare whisper in the silence. Another flood of searing cold swept through me. "Thou hast no right."

"You're Muse." I said.

"As thou seest me." She clasped her hands together in front of her, demurely.

"And this is your diary."

A sulky, nearly imperceptible nod.

I could hardly stand still, for wanting to pepper her with questions. Yet she radiated such an air of petulance, I got the impression that she would not be forthcoming. I'd never spoken to a ghost before— probably best to treat her like a demon, and choose my words carefully.

"Why does the Nalusa Falaya seek you?"

She shook her head. "I know not of ...*Falaya*." She said much more, but I couldn't catch it. Her voice, faint to begin with, seemed to fade away at times.

I showed her the entry she'd written in the book of psalms. "Who was this man?"

"No man...spirit...forest," she answered. And then, "*Lover.*"

Her anguish washed over me, mixed with shame, regret and anger. I understood that she was bound to this place against her will. She had died here, I realized. Inside her stepmother's burial crypt, yet her name was not carved into the marble. She could not leave. Maybe Blix was right and she killed herself. "What happened to you?"

Anger. Her hands went to her throat. "*Bound here...suffering.*" The rest of the story tumbled out in a series of psychic sendings. I caught a glimpse of Edmond Penfield's angry confrontation with the Elders of the nearby Senequois village, as he accused one of the men of despoiling his daughter. An image of the Elders and her father spying on the two lovers as they lay together—a snakelike creature of smoke and shadows lying between the legs of the willing girl. The shocked and somber expressions of the Elders when they told Edmond the girl was doomed—her Senequois blood had made her a target. The Nalusa Falaya, sworn enemy of the People, had taken Muse for his lover—their spawn would destroy all life.

I saw twenty of the oldest members of the Senequois tribe sacrifice themselves to bait the trap.

The blood and souls of the twenty were mixed into the earth surrounding the root ball of a sapling yew, and in an ancient ceremony, the Elders awoke the spirit within the young tree. *Plant the tree in your burial grounds, they told him. Have the girl help you dig the hole. Place a lock of her hair in the bottom of the hole. Edmond did as they suggested, telling Muse that the tree was a tribute to both her mothers.*

When next she met her lover in the woods, the Muse took him to the family plot to show him the sapling. How quickly it had grown, she marveled, but he was not interested. As he took her into his arms beneath the young tree, the Shaman, spying on her from inside Evelyn's crypt, chanted the words to awaken the tree. The lovers, distracted by their passion, did not see the clinging white threads emerge from the tree and latch onto the demon. Too late, the girl realizes what is happening and watches in horror as the tree pulls her lover inside and closes around him, sealing him away from her forever.

I saw it all as if in a movie, while she wept and raged at the injustice of it all. I felt her shame when she realized the men had been watching them together. Spying on her. She raced to her stepmother's tomb to confront them.

More than three centuries had passed since the day the Nalusa Falaya had been sealed inside the spirit tree, and yet her feelings for the demon hadn't changed. Unrepentant, the Muse remained the same, sulky, angry, child-woman she had been that day. The two prisons within sight of each other, yet the prisoners never again to be together. A tragic fate, but not one to be tampered with.

I couldn't help but feel a teeny bit sorry for her. She'd lost her birth mother, her stepmother, and through no fault of her own, become an outcast of both her tribe and the white settlement. In her misery, she'd been seduced and cursed by her own people. It wasn't fair, but it did explain much of the torment I felt in the girl's spirit. I thought of Rhys trapped inside the spirit tree and understood. A sudden inspiration though tore through me.

"Tell me," I commanded. "How do I open the spirit tree? Is it in this book?"

She gave me a sly glance. "A spirit tree consumes spirit. Only a great offering of souls will tempt the tree to open."

Something about the way she said it bothered me. Had she been human, I would have smelled a lie. Could ghosts lie? I wasn't certain, but she seemed to know more than she was saying.

I thought of all the souls trapped inside the wooden dolls that the Fewkes had used to open the spirit tree at the ritual, and my heart sank. There was no spell book. No Grimoire. The Fewkes had merely made an offering of trapped souls as bait for the tree. The diary was useless.

"There will be no such sacrifice." As I said it, I wondered how Fewkes intended to open the tree without another offering of souls. A chilling thought. "There must be another way."

From her mind, I caught a fleeting image of the Nalusa Falaya, surrounded in a cloud of will-o-the-wisps--eternal souls, trapped within its smoky coils, a vengeful creature, bent on destruction. Charlie had told me that the demon's jealousy of the Senequois people had imbued it with a thirst for revenge. If that was true, the Nalusa Falaya had never loved the Muse. Like a cat toying with a mouse, the girl had never been anything other than a future victim. Three hundred years was the blink of an eye to an immortal. It wanted her soul. And not just hers. Over the past three centuries, the Senequois clan had nearly died out; only a few people of Senequois ancestry remained.

I thought back to the moment when the Nalusa Falaya had been pulled inside the tree. There had been no sacrifice of souls on that day, only the chanting of the Elders from inside Evelyn Penfield's crypt. A surge of adrenaline coursed through me. The Muse's real mother had been an Elder shaman. As her apprentice, of course the girl would have been taught the secrets of creating a spirit tree—and opening it.

My heart skipped a beat. She would not have needed to write down the words used to open the tree.

She knew them by heart. Not only that, but she had been right there when the tree was opened.

The Muse was lying.

CHAPTER 16

I CLOSED THE book and re-wrapped it within the oiled leather doeskin. I traced the embossed designs with my finger and sought the stillness within me, as Master Foo had taught me. It would not serve my purpose to let her see my desperation.

"You know the spell the Elders used to trap the Nalusa Falaya inside the tree." I kept my voice steady. "You can open it."

She pouted. "Why should I help thee? I am spirit now, neither of this world or the next."

While I could sense some of her emotions, I wasn't sure she'd be able to tell if I lied to her. "As your lover yearns for you, I yearn for mine. He is now imprisoned inside the tree. We are sisters in our suffering." As I said it, I knew it was true in the most cosmic way. In the entire universe, only the ghost of this young girl held the key to freeing Rhys. I had to persuade her to help me.

Her eyes gleamed brighter. "He yearns for me?"

"He begged me to find you." No lie there. "Do you remember the words?"

She frowned. "It is the song in my veins. Telling thee will do no good. None but thee may hear my words."

A sliver of hope raised my spirits. "Teach me the words that I might say them."

"The spirit tree will respond only to blood or the voice of the People. As I am, I have neither. Oh please," she reached for me and I winced as her icy fingers caressed my cheek. Her words faded in and out like a radio with bad reception. "I pine for him so. It was always and ever him."

Yuck. I tried to keep in mind that she had been a girl in the throes of her first romantic love—she had been lonely. An outcast of sorts. Who knew how the creature had appeared to her, or what he'd said to woo her? The only thing I knew for sure was that the Muse had been naïve. Perhaps she still was.

It made sense that only the Senequois would have the power to command the spirit tree. Unfortunately, there weren't many descendants of the Senequois tribe remaining. There was Charlie, of course. He'd had been a shaman of the People in his day, but he was Morta's creature now, not exactly human anymore. And Honey Briscoe. Her ancestors might have even known the Penfields. She admitted as much when she told me she was a Penfield witch. She'd be perfect, but I had no way to get hold of her, as she and her boys were in protective custody. Rhys had been studying the tribe's history, but since he was now at the center of the tribe's curse, I couldn't very well ask him. And he wasn't Senequois, anyway.

"Help me," she said, her voice pleading in my mind. "I am trapped within this empty place ...only you..."

Her voice faded as her anxiety increased. In a flash of sudden insight, I realized that the Muse's grief and the curse of the Nalusa Falaya upon the Senequois people had been put in front me to solve. It was all connected somehow, to me. All the way back from the goddess Morta herself, there was no else who could break this curse, save for the Hand of Fate. From my great grandmother's kidnapping, to her coming to America, her legacy, even my own incestuous birth.

And in my mind's eye, for a single moment, everything became clear--the path though was obvious. There were patterns I could see now. It was almost as if the answer had always been there. Time didn't matter. Past, present and future were all connected, and they always had been. I knew what to do. I knew the answer.

"*As it always will be,*" whispered a voice in my head. Morta's voice.

The Muse was beginning to fade. I had to think fast. "Look, if I help you, will you open the tree?"

"Thou would reunite us?"

"You could be together," I agreed. "Forever."

She frowned. "It is a trick," she said. "As my father and the People betrayed me, so will thee."

"I'm the only one who can help you. I give you my word, as Morta's hand. You will be reunited with your lover. Do as I ask and I will make it happen, I swear it." This time, as I said it, I felt the words change my fate. Again. Something so strong I could almost taste it. A change in the air around us. Another weight upon my soul. This time, it didn't sit right.

The Muse was not convinced.

CHAPTER 17

THE SKY ABOVE the eastern horizon was growing pale when I finally got home. It had taken me all night to get the Muse to agree to help me, and I wasn't certain she would cooperate when the time came. I wasn't exactly confident that a ghost's promise held the same weight as an oath from the living. Too late for that now, I'd already given her my word, and if I screwed up, there would be other lives at stake. If I was ever going to get Rhys out of that tree, I would need help—lots of it.

The warmth of the overheated house felt like a balm to my soul. Chilled to the bone and hungry, I couldn't decide whether I wanted sleep or food first. I never had a chance to decide, because Lance was waiting up for me.

"The cards don't work," he said, his tone accusing.

He'd moved the Vic into the dining room. I went

into the dimly-lit parlor and held my hands out to the radiator, savoring the heat. "Nice to see you too, Lance. Can't this wait a few hours?" My eyes were gritty from lack of sleep.

"I've been trying for hours. The cards don't speak to me. You're going to have to do it, Sis."

"No way—I'm beat." My bedroom was just at the top of the stairs. So close. "I don't know anything about those cards. More importantly—and I cannot say this strongly enough," I glared at him. "I don't want to."

"Well we can't always get what we want, now, can we? We both know you're gonna say yes, Matt, so let's quit arguing about it get on with it."

I stifled a yawn. He was right, of course. "Oh cripes. Okay, you win. But I'm going to need you to do something for me. Something big."

He pulled me into a bear-hug. "There's my girl."

I pulled him tighter to me. He was nothing more than bones wrapped in sinew now.

Then my brother took me by the elbow and sat me down at Madame Coumlie's reading table in front of the big picture window. This was only the second time I'd ever sat here, the first being the day Rhys had introduced me to her. A deep purple tablecloth, embroidered with occult symbols worked in silver thread, covered the small table. Across the surface lay the scattered tiles of my great-grandmother's ancient ivory tarot deck.

Lance took a seat opposite, his expression wan. He mixed up the tiles by sliding them across the surface, and then gathered them up into an uneven sort of deck. "Take it. I've shuffled them, I'll tell you what to do."

His desperation, so recently reflected in the Muse's spectral image, hit me like a blow. How could I say no? Some oaths are unspoken. Lance's fate and mine were linked in a way that transcended the physical—it was primal.

Using a technique I'd learned from Master Foo, I made a conscious effort to release my frustration, anger and fear and opened myself to the lesson.

As soon as I touched the deck, a roaring sound filled my ears. The tiles were warm—hot. I tried to pull my hand away, but the deck of cards slipped *into* my body, and the little door in my mind linking me to Morta's world was blown wide open.

I rode a crest of blackest light, in darkness so bright I could hardly see. Pinwheels of color whirled before me, loosing fractal strands of questing threads out into every corner of the universe. I was above it all, while at the same time floating suspended within the streams—a vision too grand to comprehend.

Lifeline threads of every color flew and ducked and dodged and wove around me. Every color distracted me—every form and shape appeared new and unknown, whirling so fast, I struggled to make sense of the pattern.

I don't know how long I floated there, as the universe unfolded, baring its secrets to me. I saw the creation of everything—all was chaos, and yet...

Soul threads merged and unraveled or broke, then wove together with other soul threads—some matching, some not, and the fabric spun into a new direction, the strands always moving.

I nodded my approval, feeling like some ancient seamstress, as the design blossomed within the loom of time and space. The threads grew into a fabric stretching beyond my comprehension and I felt an inner satisfaction in the work, even as blemishes appeared and threads frayed. I snipped a thread or two, my shears snicking and gleaming in my left hand, while with my right, I scattered the ivory cards across the cosmic fabric of the universe.

Through Morta's eyes, I saw her as she saw me—now come into possession of my full powers as the Oracle of Fate. I anticipated every twist of the thread, every frayed end. Time and the universe ebbed and flowed, and the thread of every soul connected to every other. I saw it all—even the slimmest, most fragile twist.

Everything is connected. Every one of us. I saw it all. All that is new becomes old and is then woven again as new in a kaleidoscopic tapestry of patterns, spanning time and space into infinity.

There. I turned my attention to an especially appealing swirl in the pattern—Shore Haven. A special place, the threads gleamed darkly in starlight, I spotted a tangle in the weaving. I stretched my hand out, longing to smooth away the imperfection, but Morta's cold fingers stopped me.

Do not presume, Oracle, to attempt what even the Goddess of Fate has no power to change. You are the harbinger; your brother is the wheel. As it has been, so it shall be again.

Nooo, I screamed, my voice lost in the roar of silence. *Help me, Morta!*

Her whispered voice spoke through my bones. *You have everything you need, if only you would see...*

CHAPTER 18

WHEN I OPENED my eyes, I was lying on the floor with a pillow under my head and Blix sitting on my chest, looking very worried.

My mouth tasted of bile. "Where's Lance," I asked. Sun streamed through the front window. "What time is it?"

"I am glad you are awake, Mistress. Your brother left an hour ago. Are you feeling better?"

I ran my fingers through my hair. "Yeah, I think I do. How long was I out?"

"An hour. He said he had a bird to catch." Blix answered. "A robin."

I got to my feet and went into the kitchen for a glass of water. "Not a bird, a woman named Robin." The threads had shown me a very long twining between the two of them. If he chose her, she would be his truest love—his staunchest ally and partner in life. The

Lord of Luck would always have something good in his life to balance out the bad. Or, he could die, or live to have many more children with another. And Mina! His daughter could be a teacher. Or a doctor. Or drug addict...a headache pounded at my temples.

So many choices, so many threads, pinch points, and decisions. Even decisions postponed—each and every one connected to other decisions and actions and others, all in turn connected to the fate of the planet and the fabric of the cosmos.

And Rhys. My heart ached with the sudden thought of him. He could die—I could see he was close to it, now. That thread was thick with likelihood, but there were other threads, too. He could live—a hollow shell of himself, or a bitter old warrior living in his millennia of memories, or—I blushed at the thought of it; in a place of peace and laughter and happiness. I could not see myself in that future, but I knew, without being told that the Oracle cannot see her own fate. Enough to see the thread of possibility was there.

It was all there. Too many choices to determine a single outcome; be it a path to glory or the road of destruction, every soul was woven into the fabric of the universe. I knew it, now. Like I knew my own name. Destiny is not the end—spirit is eternal.

I gulped down a glassful of water.

"Blix, what did I say to Lance?"

Blix told me I'd babbled a little at the beginning,

but repeated what I'd said verbatim. "Like the wheel, you must travel. Like the wheel, the longer you stay in one place, the more you use up the good and bring the bad back around to you and those you love. Keep moving, and you can stay ahead of the curve. Fortuna's wheel embedded in your chest makes it so. Share your fortune with others, and you may linger, but the price is high. You may never rest, lest the turn of the wheel catch up with you. Fortuna's luck is the blood in your veins, but every moment of pleasure brings an equal amount of pain. It is the nature of the wheel."

Blix licked his lips.

"That was it?" It seemed to me that there was so much more to tell him. Of Mina—and Robin. The blonde witch was important—and not just to Lance. Rhys needed her as well…

My heart lurched. I needed Lance and Robin both to help me rescue Rhys. I had seen it in the threads. There were others, too. I wasn't sure who or why, but Lance and Robin had to be there.

"Aye, Mistress. Your brother seemed well pleased. He put the pillow under your head before he left and asked me to watch over you."

"Where did he go?"

"To see his daughter, he said. He took your motorcycle. I do not believe he will be gone long."

The tension in my shoulders eased. "You did a fine job, Blix. I am well pleased."

Blix narrowed his eyes at me; a cat-like mannerism that I knew meant he was content. "I sense a change in you, Mistress."

The water had refreshed me. I flicked my right wrist and the small deck of ivory cards slipped into the palm of my hand. Son of a gun. I flicked my blackened hand and my shears appeared in my left. "Not even Madame Coumlie had both of these. I guess I really am the Hand of Fate, now."

Blix leapt up onto his favorite spot at the top of one of the bookshelves. "The Hand of Fate was merely a title. You have come into your power. You are the Oracle, now."

I flicked my wrists again and both the shears and deck of cards disappeared. *Cool.* "Yeah, but what does it mean?"

Blix waggled his ears, a sign of amusement. "I am not the Oracle, Mistress. Only you can decide."

CHAPTER 19

AFTER CHECKING MY messages, I called Sheriff Reynolds first.

"Where the hell have you been, Deputy?" That he didn't use my name was telling.

"Doing my job," I answered, truthfully. "Where are you?"

"We got a solid tip that Fewkes would be at the cult compound last night. We raided the place at dawn, but they outfoxed us. Fewkes wasn't there. Nor was our missing man, Cusick. We made a dozen arrests, but place had already been cleaned out. Not a single cell phone found, and all the computers had had their hard drives removed. We found a shredder, though. It was full of what looked like financial documents. It'll take a while, but we'll find the cult's assets. Just a matter of time."

"The agent that was killed at Knutt's Apple Farm,"

I said. "What was his name?"

"Why do you want to know?"

"I guess it doesn't really matter," I said. I could see the pattern. A revenge of staggering proportions. "The Nalusa Falaya is slaking its thirst for revenge on the indigenous peoples of North America. The agent who was killed—his ancestors were members of the Tuscarora nation. All of the Nalusa Falaya's victims are of Native American descent. As is Hugo Green."

There was a long pause. "You can't know that. No one knows that. Tell me you've got the book."

"It's in a safe place. Fewkes can't get to it."

"Good, because the Feds have already set up the exchange. They're doing it tonight."

"I'm not giving the Feds the book, Jimbo. It won't do them any good."

"They don't need the book. They never needed it. It's bait to set the trap for Fewkes."

"You can't be serious," I said. "When Fewkes realizes you don't have the book, he'll call in the demon."

"It's going down, Deputy. It's not our show."

"At least tell Green to stay out of it," I begged, knowing as I said it, that nothing would dissuade Agent Green from carrying out his plan to capture Fewkes. "If he's there, he'll be in danger. Everywhere Fewkes goes, the Nalusa Falaya won't be far away. If the demon shows up, it'll be a bloodbath."

"Yeah, I'll be sure to pass along your suggestion."

The Sheriff's voice dripped with sarcasm. "Look these guys have taken down demon masters before. When they take down Fewkes, the smoke monster will be a non-issue. They know what they're doing. They're pretty confident."

I knew better than to ask Reynolds where and when it would go down. Fewkes would demand neutral ground, a place of his choosing. In my mind's eye, I saw an abandoned warehouse in an industrial area. I could see how it would all go down. Midnight. I saw the snipers with their ketamine dart rifles, and a neurotoxin on the book cover. Gas grenades, with flamethrowers as a backup. Messy—and doomed to fail.

Vampires would have a better chance.

Hmmm. With Fewkes distracted by his desire for the book, maybe I could use that to my advantage. Not much time to pull things together, but it might work. For the first time in weeks, the drums started thrumming in my veins.

"Stay out of it, Blackman. That's an order." Sometimes, I swear Sheriff Reynolds is prescient.

I grinned. "Yes Sir. Wouldn't dream of it." I could hardly stand still.

I ordered Blix to shadow Agent Green and let me know where the meeting would be. Meanwhile, I had places to go, things to do, people to see.

A djenie to save.

CHAPTER 20

I CALLED LANCE and told him to meet me in the parking lot at the Pittsford Wegmans. When he pulled up on the Vic, I briefly laid out about my plan to rescue Rhys. To my surprise, Lance immediately agreed to help. I swapped him the keys to Trusty Rusty and gave him a list of what I needed. "Pick up Charlie Crimmer and meet me at the apple farm at ten tonight. Dress warm."

"What are you going to do until then?" he asked.

"I've got some favors to call in."

Once Lance was gone, I swung my leg over the Vic, and headed north, toward Penfield and Growlers Pub. It was dark by the time I got there, but still Happy Hour.

Well, maybe not happy. When I opened the front door, the jukebox was eerily silent. Only the occasional clack of a cueball and the thud of balls sinking in the pocket broke the silence. I scanned the bar, ignored by the regulars, most of whom I now recognized. The one person I most wanted to talk to wasn't there.

I walked over to the bar to speak to Kevin. When I told him that the FBI had raided the cult compound and made a dozen arrests, he perked right up. "That's great news," he said. I stopped him before he could make a public announcement.

"Nash Redleaf and the others weren't killed because they were lycans. Nash was killed because he is a descendant of the Senequois people." I told him about the Native American connection to the Nalusa Falaya. "He's targeting them. Not just the Senequois, but all Native People. He's using Fewkes to lure them to him."

Kevin paled as the truth of my words struck home. "Race, sex, creed, or religion, it doesn't matter. Pack trumps all. Tell me what you need."

"I've got a plan, but there isn't much time. It has to happen tonight. I need a couple of guys with strong backs." I told him what and who I wanted.

To my great relief, he agreed, and started making calls.

My next stop was the Orpheus Mortuary in Webster. Although still early by vampire standards, I knew Neldene and her husband Enrique would have been up since dusk.

Neldene greeted me wearing a white velvet

bathrobe. She kissed me on the cheek and shushed me when I tried to apologize for intruding. "It's been too long, Mattie. It's wonderful to see you."

She brought me back through the Funeral Parlor and into her and Enrique's private quarters. The décor was comfortable and tasteful, much like what I knew of Neldene's taste—a neutral palette with a variety of textures. A large canvas portrait of Neldene and Enrique on their wedding day hung over the fireplace. We chatted for a few minutes, but she could sense my impatience.

I don't care what anyone says about vampires. In my experience, they have been some of the kindest, most civil people I've ever met. Yeah, they drink human blood, but not without permission from the donor. They have contracts and everything. It's nothing like in the movies.

"What is it dear? You're as fidgety as ferret with fleas. How can I help?"

"I'm sorry," I began, "I don't have much time. I am looking for a particular vampire, but my djemon cannot seem to find him. I was hoping you might know where he, um, dwells—er, how I can get hold of him."

She gave me a knowing smile. "Some of us are better than others in keeping our secrets. Who are you seeking?"

"The dance instructor, Maestro."

"Oh..." She gave me a worried look. "Well. He is

not really one of us," she said, as if uncertain how to proceed. "Not all vampires are the same--."

"Yes, I know. He and Stella feed on emotions, not blood. I went by his studio, but it's closed tonight. I really need to speak to him tonight."

"Oh dear," she said. "I do not have permission to reveal that information. Believe me when I say this; he is not one to take kindly to strangers. His appetites—I mean, his kind does not respond well to surprises."

"I am not a stranger," I told her. "Rhys and I are, well, I mean, he knows us—me. I have a business proposition for him. It's a private matter, but there's a time element involved. I'm hoping he'll be interested."

Her eyes widened in understanding. "I will let him know where to meet you."

Forty minutes later, I was seated in the basement of the Amble Inn, my hands wrapped around a cup of hot coffee, making my case to the dance instructor.

He was impeccably dressed, as usual, but did not seem particularly pleased to see me. I gave him a brief outline of the FBI plan to lure John Fewkes into an ambush. "The deal going down tonight. There will be a storm of emotions present."

He gave me a dismissive shrug. "What makes you think this human scheme will be of any interest to me?"

I didn't have time to dance around the topic. "Rhys and I have taken your Tango Jive class. We know what you are. Your kind feeds off powerful emotions. Lust, for one." I shrugged, as if it didn't matter to me one way or another. A blush warmed my cheeks. "I wanted to thank you for that gift. You introduced us to a new kind of music." *A beat that stirs my blood and compels me to action like nothing else.*

He raised his eyebrows, as if to say, *whatever.* "I was led to believe this was a business proposition."

"I thought perhaps you might get tired of a diet of lust."

He said nothing.

"What if I could offer you a feast of emotions?" I paused, uncertain. "Fear, for one, with a bit of rage mixed in."

"Fear," he scoffed. "Only children truly experience fear on a regular basis, and I choose not to exploit their undeveloped emotions. By the time they are adults, true fear has been blunted to mere stress. In my youth, the battlefield was my milieu. These days, I prefer lust."

"Fair enough," I countered. "But the same meal every day would dull even the most discriminating palate, does it not? I'm offering you a smorgasbord, with a cherry of betrayal on top." I didn't wait for his answer, I simply handed him the address of the warehouse that Blix had given me. "At midnight tonight, Federal agents will attempt to capture an immortal sorcerer. Against his will, he is enslaved to a demon and desperate to get his hands on a book they will be using as bait. He believes the book will free him. When he discovers the trap, it will push him over the edge. All I am asking is that you feed on that fury and slow him down enough for the Feds to get their hands on him. I am certain the sorcerer's well of emotions will provide feast enough for both you and Stella."

I couldn't read the Maestro at all.

"You think I would do the bidding of the Hand of Fate?" He nodded. "Yes, I knew who you were from the moment you and your lover walked into my studio. Let me tell you something. I answer to no man. Or woman, either, save for Stella, no matter who or what she may be. You are asking me to risk exposure among a swarm of federal agents; and for what? A meal? I dine as often as I please. I have a special arrangement with an angel investor and his consortium, which will provide a rich future for Stella and I. In two years I shall be living like a king. What can you possibly offer me if I do this thing for you?"

I didn't think I had any more promises to give. No more oaths to swear. "What do you want that I have the power to give you?"

At that moment, Stella sashayed into the room. She must've been listening from the stairwell. She wore stiletto heels and a pair of skin-tight silver lace leggings. A bustier of glittery silver lace emphasized her amazing hourglass figure. She leaned over and whispered something into Maestro's ear. The corners of his eyes wrinkled in delight—a true smile graced his too-smooth features.

"Yes, that would be lovely." He stood, his arm around Stella's trim waist, as he pulled her close. "Every year, Stella and I invite as select group of influential friends to the studio for a dance recital, featuring some of our most-gifted long-time students. This year, our patron investor and several members of his ah, inner circle will be in the audience. While we would not normally extend an invitation to you and Rhys, Stella has persuaded me to make an exception. We would very much like you and your handsome beau to attend." He chuckled. "I am certain he would relish meeting you."

There was no mistaking their intent. Obviously, Maestro and Stella were not the only vamps who fed off strong emotions. They wanted me to allow their friends to feed off the lust that Rhys and I shared." Ick. I shook my head. "It's not really my thing. And I'm not sure I can speak for Rhys," I said. "He's kind of.... I mean, he might not be—."

"Tut-tut, my dear," Stella cooed. "Of course Maestro and I will give your sorcerer a try. And in return, we will expect you both at the studio on Valentines night."

She turned from Maestro, her heels clicking against the cement floor. At the stairs, she turned and raised an eyebrow at me, her expression sly. "Don't disappoint me, youngling. I like to play with my food." The two of them stepped lightly up the stairs to the bar.

Oh cripes, what have I done?

I swallowed the lump in my throat and waited, hoping they wouldn't linger in the bar. The basement suddenly seemed claustrophobic. I'd always liked Stella, but now I wasn't so sure. Of the two, she now seemed more dangerous. Or perhaps that not-so-subtle threat was her way of triggering an emotional snack from me.

Tick tock.

I didn't have time to dwell on it—Valentine's Day was light years away, as far as I was concerned. Time enough to think about it later. The drums in my head were calling me. Time to go.

CHAPTER 21

I CRUISED INTO the parking lot of Knutt's Apple Farm, the Vic warm and rumbling beneath me. Lance and Charlie stood amid a small group of people at the far end of the lot, near a couple of pickup trucks and a horse trailer. A mule was getting unloaded from the trailer. I parked the Vic next to Trusty Rusty and joined them. Robin, the ward witch from Toronto, stayed closed to Lance.

I approached the guy with the mule, stopping short as the animal flicked its ears back. It was a big—a lot bigger than I expected. "You must be Terry," I said. "Thank you for coming."

"Least I could do," he said. His square jaw held a tell-tale lump of tobacco. A shock of dark hair peeked out from beneath his lumberjack cap. "Chief Halliday told me what you did for me. I appreciate it." His hands constantly stroked the neck of the edgy mule.

He had not been at his best when I arrested him—at the midway point between wolf and human.

"What'd she do?" Charlie asked, as he stepped up beside me. The mule flicked its ears forward.

"She let the right people know where I was so I didn't have to spend the night in jail," he answered. "You know mules, old man?"

"Been a long time." Charlie's voice had gone soft, a tone I'd only heard when he spoke to his djemon, Annie. He held still as the mule gave him a suspicious sniff. "Who is this beauty?"

"This is Adelaide," Terry answered, with no little pride. He tightened the girth strap on the mule's saddle. "And that's my brother Neil over there, hitching Nosey up the travois."

The black mule, Nosey, stood patiently as Neil buckled the sled to its pack harness. The travois frame was constructed from of a pair of long, hollow metal poles, fastened to straps on either side of the mule's pack. The poles met at a point behind the mule at a single wheel, like a reverse wheelbarrow. Terry explained that the cart was used for packing game out of rough country, but they'd added a sling and strapped a couple of down sleeping bags, to keep the victim warm on the way back.

The victim.

"Don't worry," Terry said. He patted the mule's flank. "These are our best hunting mules. Smart and ornery enough to stand their ground against a bear, or even cougar. They've never faced a demon, but I wouldn't want to go up against one without 'em. You'll be safe, believe me."

Charlie rubbed the mule's lower jaw. "I can see that that," he cooed. The mule leaned in to his touch. "Hope she don't mind carryin' an old man."

Terry grinned. "Adelaide doesn't usually take to strangers, but I think she may make an exception in your case."

"I think we'll get on just fine," Charlie answered. "Had me one, once," he said, running his hand along the creature's neck. "This is a fine lookin' animal. Good character."

Terry grinned. "You know your mules, sir." He introduced the other two men, Luke, and Roland. Luke was the oldest lycan I'd ever seen. Lycans don't age like humans do, and Luke's physique was no less imposing than the other pack members, but Luke's close-cropped hair was silver—he could have been anywhere between sixty to ninety years old. Roland, on the other hand, looked like a Mr. Universe on steroids; his clothes pulled tight across his chest and thighs.

Both men had been recommended to me by the pack's new Alpha, Chief Treyson Halliday.

Roland wrinkled up his nose at the sight of Robin. "Nobody said anything about a witch coming along."

"Cool it, Rolly." Neil said. "This is a rescue mission,

not a rumble."

"She's not from around here," Lance warned. "She's not a cult member."

The invisible connection between Lance and the ward witch positively glowed. Cool. If this was part of my new powers, I liked it a lot.

"One witch is as bad as another, in my book." Roland jerked his head in the direction of his tricked-out, jacked-up Silverado. "Those are brand-new tires, babe. If they get slashed tonight, I'm taking it out of your hide."

"Knock it off," I said, in my best Deputy Blackman voice. "When I asked for volunteers, Robin stepped forward, same as you. We can't do this thing without her—or any of you. Even if we do everything right, there's no guarantee that this will work or that Rhys will still be alive. And nobody knows how the demon will react—it could kill us all."

Their anxiety hit me like a wave. Maybe mentioning the demon wasn't such a good idea, but I wanted to remind everyone of what we were up against. I thought of Maestro and Stella and hoped they would be able to weaken John Fewkes at the FBI's ambush. The only way either plan could work was if we could keep the two immortals apart. "The Nalusa Falaya is immortal. It can't be killed, so don't waste your time trying— you'll just end up pissing it off. As it happens, we can't free Rhys without the demon's presence."

Roland's smirk deepened into a sneer. "Little bitty thing like her will probably pee her panties when the action starts."

"Shut up, Rolly," Neil and Luke said, in unison.

"You know I'm right," the muscle-bound lycan refused to back down. "She'll be in the way."

If Chief Halliday hadn't already told me that Roland's heroism in retrieving wounded soldiers in the heat of battle had earned him the respect of every man in his unit, I would have asked him to leave right there.

"As it happens," I put my arm around Robin's shoulders. "This witch holds the key to everyone's safety. If things go south, and the demon comes after you, get to the crypt. It's heavily warded—the Nalusa Falaya won't be able to get inside."

Rolly said nothing, but his eyes widened with new respect.

"All of the demon's attention should be on Charlie, Robin and me," I said. "All you guys have to do is help Lance get Rhys out of that tree, loaded onto the travois, and get him out of here. After the tree opens, I don't know how much time you'll have," I swallowed past the lump in my throat. I had to believe that Rhys was still alive. "No matter what you see or hear, keep your attention on Lance." I gave my brother a weak smile. "He's always been pretty lucky at getting out of scrapes. It's what he does best."

"What are you gonna to do?" Roland asked me.

"She's going to do what *she* does best," Lance said. "She's gonna piss off the demon so bad, he won't even notice little old us." He gave me a mock salute.

Everybody had a good laugh at that one.

Over Charlie's protests that he didn't need any help, Terry and his brother got Charlie up into Adelaide's saddle and we headed out through the orchards. There was no moon—only the cold light of winter stars reflected off the snow lit our path. Terry had the lead, walking at Adelaide's head, breaking trail through the knee-deep snow while his brother Neil led Nosey, pulling the travois behind. Roland followed Neil, followed by Luke, Lance, and Robin. I brought up the rear, watching the lifelines of everyone in the party flare and dim as they considered the job ahead.

Roland hadn't been totally wrong about Robin. Of all of us, she worried me the most. Her aura was soft— to me, her power felt like peace and light and spring and green things growing. I doubt she'd ever raised her voice in anger. As much as I hated Roland's assessment of her, I wasn't sure she wouldn't freak out when the Nalusa Falaya showed up. The lycans were battle-hard veterans. They had all served in the Middle East. They'd come through battles, unimaginable weirdness and pain, and survived. Terry and his brother had grown up hunting wild game. I felt confident they would be steady when things fell apart.

Lance would fine. He had Fortuna's luck to protect him. It was the reason I'd asked him to lead the rescue. I knew he wasn't wild about Rhys, and maybe he hadn't served his country in battle like the others, but he'd seen things. Done things—and he was no rookie when it came to demons.

Of course, Lance had been riding Fortuna's wave of luck for a while. It could turn at any time. We couldn't put this off any longer. I chewed my thumbnail. There was so much that could go wrong. That had already gone wrong. What if I was wrong again? What if Robin couldn't break the ward on the crypt? What if Fewkes saw through the FBI trap and didn't take the bait?

Everything hinged on that. In my vision, I'd seen that the only path to success was to separate Fewkes and the Nalusa Falaya and hit them at the same time. *What if...?*

We cleared the orchards and began the climb. Charlie lay low over the saddle, clinging to Adelaide's neck as the mule bucked up the steep hill. For a two-hundred year-old shaman, Charlie is in pretty good shape, but there was no way he could have managed a mile in deep snow over uneven ground and up that hill to the cemetery on his own. We crested the knoll above the cemetery and paused, the mules snorting plumes of steam into the chill night air.

The reflected starlight against the whiteness of the snowy vale brought out details almost as clear as day.

I pointed out the spirit tree the bottom of the vale, and the copse of firs clustered around Evelyn Penfield's white marble crypt, halfway up the hill to the right. "Charlie, Robin and I will be at the crypt," I said. "If all goes as planned, we'll take that path down to the spirit tree." I pointed to the faint depression in the snow which led down into the vale and the tumbled ruins of the three altars near the base of the spirit tree. "I think you guys will be safe enough behind the altars, until we can get the spirit tree open."

Terry helped Charlie out of the saddle, and pointed out a dark stand of trees on the far side of the cemetery. "Neil and I will be over there with mules. He'll bring Adelaide when you're ready."

I gave Neil a questioning look. "You're leaving?"

"No, I drew the short straw," he explained. "I'm going to be with Nosey and the travois. Our mom will kill us if anything happens to Nosey. He's her favorite."

"Of course," I said, amused that this macho hunter-warrior feared his mother's ire. "When battling demons, always protect your mom's favorite mule. Makes perfect sense." A faint drumbeat started up in the back of my head, and I grinned. This was going to work. It felt right. "Let's do this."

Lance handed me a walkie-talkie handset and I checked to make sure it worked. "Once you have Rhys, get him out of here. Don't wait for us."

"Don't worry, Matt" he said, with a furtive glance

at Robin. "I've got this. Get that tree open and keep the demon off us. We'll get him out, I promise." He chucked me under the chin and headed down toward the spirit tree.

Robin and I helped Charlie toward the crypt. Now that we were here, that little drumbeat gave me a boost of confidence. With Lance's luck and the lycan's muscle, we were as ready as we could be.

At the entrance to the Penfield tomb, Robin ran her hands around the entrance. "There's a story here," she said, after a long moment. "So much pain and betrayal." She turned to Charlie. "And sacrifice. "

Charlie also examined the open doorway, but did not touch the cold marble. "Yep," he nodded, his chin jutted forward in an expression I recognized as anger. His dark eyes glinted in the starlight. "This is death magic. I know of it, but I've never seen anything like it. A murdered soul is bound here."

My stomach did a little flip. The Muse implied that she'd committed suicide.

"Yes," Robin agreed. "With great violence, by someone she knew. So intricate," She wiped her hands on her jacket. "There are threads here which connect to the souls of the Senequois people who sacrificed themselves to create the spirit tree." She waved her arm towards the rim of the vale, around us. "Their remains are buried around the rim of this vale, and connected by ward threads to the spirit tree and this tomb. To remove this ward would negate the sacrifice of the men and women of Charlie's clan." She frowned. "It's a web. If I break the ward, it will kill the tree."

"It's not a ward," Charlie explained. "It is a soul-keep—a curse, to use the white man's terms. The magic here keeps the soul trapped inside the tree from ever leaving. If broken, the spirit of the Senequois girl will be free to cross into the land of the dead." He made an unhappy face.

I thought about the story the tortured ghost girl had told me. "What's the harm in that? It's the way of things—you taught me that, Charlie."

"No." Charlie grimaced. "It cannot be. Not for her. She is anchored here."

"He's right," Robin agreed. "It does feel more like a curse than a ward. It carries a warning—the soul within the tomb keeps an evil spirit chained to this place. They're linked. If the soul is released, the demon will be loosed upon the world." She shuddered in her parka. "I've never felt anything like it."

"The demon is already loose. We're trying to recapture it. The Muse can't open the spirit tree unless she can leave the crypt."

"Let me try to explain." Robin slipped her gloves back on. "Tribal blood magic binds the Nalusa Falaya to this geographical area. It's old magic. Unchangeable. Ancient. It's in the stones and rocks and everything that grows here. In the more recent past, the tribal magic was refreshed by the blood and souls of Senequois men and women who sacrificed themselves to create the spirit tree. A few drops of the landowner's blood added to the soil around the tree when it was planted, bound the landowner and the tree to the land of that ancient Senequois legacy. It created a unique binding that was new and powerful—and not wholly of the People."

"Edmond Penfield," I said. "You're saying a white man willingly participated in a Senequois ritual? Why would he?"

"The Penfields and the People were friends," Charlie said. "Seeing his stepdaughter in the arms of an evil demon must have driven him nearly mad. The idea that the Nalusa Falaya could seduce other young girls and spread his evil seed would have helped the shaman convince him that the spirit tree was the only way to contain the demon."

It was all connected. The girl had been a nothing but a plaything for the Nalusa Falaya. They'd used her to trap him.

"So why would he—wait." I stepped into the vault, intending to confront the Muse. I caught a glimpse of her pale form as she swept into me. I fell to my knees, overcome by the anger and shame of a young girl—she was so young! So angry. The vision came to me as a memory—her memory.

As the tree engulfs her lover, she races up the hill

in terror, seeking the sanctuary and solace of her stepmother's crypt. Instead, she finds her stepfather is there, bristling with rage. So too, are several of her elder clansmen, their expressions dark with rebuke and accusation. She screams, reaching for Edmond, seeking to scratch his eyes out. He'd criticized her, spied on her, and now he'd gotten the elders of her own clan to take away the only man she would ever love.

He ruined everything. How dare he look at her like that...?

Edmond wraps his hands around her neck, and, lifting her off her feet, drags her deeper into the tomb. The last sound she hears is of her own neck snapping. There is no pain, only a sense of relief as she rises from her lifeless body. She doesn't understand what has happened to her. Edmond won't listen to her, or even look at her. Eventually, the elders help the dazed and broken man to his feet. She feels nothing for him, not fully realizing what has happened. The body of the girl on the floor means something, but she cannot quite remember what. Curious, she lingers inside her mother's tomb while the shaman and her clansmen chant outside. By the time she realizes what they have done, it is too late. She cannot leave. She cannot even approach the entrance. She is trapped.

"There is too much at stake here," Robin said, as she helped me to my feet. "I will not open the soul-keep."

CHAPTER 22

IT ONLY TOOK me a moment to retrieve Muse's oilskin-wrapped journal from the corner where I'd left it for safekeeping.

"Remember thy promise," the Muse wailed, her voice pleading in my mind. "I have endured so much." The spirit of the Muse continued to moan and carry on, bouncing off the marble walls like a bee caught in a jar. A spoiled child.

"You lied to me," I said. I could order a demon to speak truth to me, but I had no control over a willful, teen-aged ghost.

"Noooo... Thee hast no mercy. I have done no wrong; only to accept the love he offered. They had no right—." She pounded her transparent chest with her fist. "It is *me* he wants!"

Yeah—no. I bit back the sour retort. I could only imagine what a handful this girl had been while alive.

Robin and Charlie had the truth of it. Arguing with her was a waste of time. And Robin already looked like she was sorry she'd come. Suddenly, the likelihood of opening the tree and rescuing Rhys seemed impossible. We needed a new plan.

My phone began to vibrate and I answered it. "Talk to me, Blix. What's happening?"

"Agent Green and his men are in place at the warehouse. The sorcerer is in the area, but has not yet shown himself. The Nalusa Falaya is with him."

"That's not good. What about Maestro and Stella? Have the vampires arrived?"

There was a long pause. "I do not sense the dance instructor and his partner as I do the Nalusa Falaya."

"What does that mean, Blix? Speak plainly." They *had* to be there. "Are they there or not?"

"Vampires smell of blood," he explained. "I smell no vampires. However, they are *not* like other vampires. I cannot say if they are here or not."

Robin kept looking toward the vale where the men were. Where Lance was.

"Thou promised we would be together," the Muse accused. "I heard what the witch said," the ghost pointed an accusing finger at Robin.

"I've got to go, Blix. Keep me posted." I put my phone back in my pocket. We didn't have much time. With Charlie as a Senequois vessel for the Muse, we'd planned to have him speak the spell a few feet from the tree, but if he passed through the wards on the entrance to the crypt, the Muse would be expelled from his body.

"You will never be together," Charlie told her. "You will never leave this place. You will never pass into Morta's realm."

"Um, Charlie," I began, but he put his hand out to silence me.

"Hush, child," he said. "What you want cannot be."

I wasn't sure if he was speaking to me or the Muse at that point. The two of them began speaking in the language of the Senequois people, something I didn't understand.

I felt the connections in my mind changing as the paths to Rhys dimmed and disappeared. I had to do something.

Robin reached out to me, gripping my hand in hers. "You told me Rhys trusted you with his death. You cannot break this curse to save him. Let him go."

I slapped the book against my thigh in frustration. What if she was right? So many lives had been lost already. "This is not just about Rhys," I said. "The only way to trap that monster is to put him back into the spirit tree, and the Muse is the only one who can open the tree." There had to be a way. "What if we leave the wards in place? Couldn't Charlie open the spirit tree from inside the vault? It's not that far." I turned to Charlie for confirmation. "Can you shout the spell?"

"I don't know," Charlie sounded doubtful. "Mebbe."

A blink of light came from the men at the altar near the spirit tree. The guys were in place. Tick tock. "Come on, I said. "Let's give it a try.

"No," the Muse answered. "I will not do it. Thou gave me thy word we would be reunited."

There had to be a way to convince her. I remembered the frigid day when Fewkes and the Nalusa Falaya had trapped Blix and me inside the vault. I'd heard someone weeping that day—it must have been her. I couldn't help but feel sorry for her; she'd been so young. She'd hardly had a chance to experience life.

"If you love him, let us help you," I said. "There is only one way to keep him near you forever, and that means sealing him back inside the spirit tree. You like knowing he is nearby, don't you? He will be safe there. You know he yearns for you," I said. "We can't unbind this place, but you can go back to the way things were. I know you don't want him to leave. His presence is a comfort for you, isn't it?"

"Yes! I long for him so." She covered her face with her hands and began to cry. Her voice faded away, and then returned as a shout. "The raven man has ruined everything!" She raised her head, her features a snarl. "I hate him!"

It took me a minute to realize who she was talking about—John Fewkes. "Yeah, well, they're tied together now." Jealousy wasn't just for the living, apparently. "The only way to protect your man from the um, raven man is with the spirit tree. Open the tree and help us put him back inside. The raven man will be forced to leave. He won't bother you any longer." I reached for every argument I could think of. "You'll be able to watch over him. You'll be at peace again. Isn't that better than losing him?"

She shook her head. "Thou just wants me to open the tree for thee. To rescue thy lover." She sounded resentful

"Yes," I answered. So okay, the Muse had died a horrible death, believing in her teen-aged heart that the Nalusa Falaya was the love of her life. That was a rotten thing, but this ghost was quickly becoming a royal pain. "I do want Rhys back. But if he dies, or if he's already dead, I know I'll accept it and be at peace, knowing that our love is eternal. Love is the cosmic truth that binds the universe together, whether my lover and I will ever be together or not."

As I said it, I knew it to be the truth. I love Rhys. He loves me. He'd told me he knew from the first day we met. It took me longer to get there, but now I knew it, too.

"I feel sorry for you," I said. There was no time left for arguing. "Your lover will never die. Eventually, he will forget about you. Maybe he already has. Sooner or later, he will leave you forever. Only you have the power to keep him close to you for eternity." I shrugged as If I didn't care. "Perhaps you did not truly love him" I twisted the knife deeper. This had to work. "He will find someone else to love, and you will spend eternity here alone. It is your choice."

She moaned. "Thee should not say that—thee cannot mean that." She faded out of sight.

"Where did she go," asked Robin.

"You ticked 'er off, girlie," Charlie said. "What do we do now?"

My phone buzzed again. It was Blix, telling me that John Fewkes and the Nalusa Falaya had entered the warehouse.

The Muse reappeared. Her demeanor had changed. She moved to stand directly in front of Charlie. "Very well," she said. "I will do it. We will be as we were. I will be at peace, knowing he will never leave me. But only him." She gave me an accusing look. "Not that awful man—the raven man."

Charlie spoke softly, laying his gnarled hand upon the Muse's spectral head as if in benediction. After a long moment, she covered her face with her hands and began to weep again. I didn't understand what Charlie and the Muse were saying—it had a rhythmic sound, like the beginning of a ceremony. Charlie picked up his hand drum and nodded. Slowly, he began to hum, beating the drum with a slow, gentle beat, like a drop of water from a faucet.

This was it. I could feel it. The time, the place, the people.

The muse circled the ceiling slowly, descending a little with every beat of the drum. Robin and I exchanged a worried glance. Now that it was about to happen, I worried for Charlie's safety. He wasn't exactly human, but that didn't mean the ghost couldn't hurt him.

The sound he made when she took possession of him was like the riffling of dry pages in an old book. He opened his eyes, but they focused inward. Once, twice, he attempted to speak, but couldn't. Then the rhythm of the drum changed, and Charlie began to hum.

It sounded a little like the chanting I'd heard him do when he cleansed a house—a melodic nasal tone, halfway between speaking and singing.

"Can you feel it," Robin asked.

"Feel what?"

"Magic." She spread out her arms, and her long blonde hair floated out, away from her body—as if filled with static electricity. "It's starting."

Without warning, Charlie dropped the drum and stood up straight, straighter than I'd ever seen him. He clasped his hands together before him, and began to sing.

But it wasn't Charlie singing.

A girl's voice, angelic and clear, filled the tomb with song; so pure, so light, so filled with yearning. Lyrical and sweet, the melody soared and floated, the words and tune unfamiliar. I gripped the Hymnal tightly. Of course.

The spell was a *song*.

My heart twisted with every note. I blinked back sudden tears at the beauty of it. It wasn't natural.

I called Blix on the cell phone. As soon as he answered, I heard gunshots. Explosions. What about the word *immortal* didn't the FBI understand?

"Alright Blix, this is it. How close are you to the action?"

"I am within a few dozen yards of the demon. As you suggested, he has ignored me, thus far."

"Yeah, well that's about to change. Put me on speaker and then get here as fast as you can fly, and don't lose him."

There was no answer. There didn't need to be. As soon as the Nalusa Falaya heard the Muse's song, I heard a roar as loud as an oncoming train. I didn't need to hear any more.

"Incoming," I said to Lance on the talkie-talkie. "Get ready." It was about all I had time for. In less than a minute, Blix swooped into the vault. Outside, the Nalusa Falaya circled above the crypt, howling in frustration.

"Muuuuuuse!"

Her song continued, louder now. After about ten minutes, I peeked outside, immediately ducking back as I glimpsed movement just outside. The Nalusa Falaya dug great gouges into the deep snow with its claws, bugling the Muse's name, over and over, like a lovesick moose.

I used the walkie-talkie to talk to Lance. "What's happening? Is the tree opening?"

"It's shaking, but other than dropping a few needles, and snow, not much else." Lance answered. "How long is this supposed to take?"

"At the ritual, it didn't take long at all. Can you hear the Muse singing?" I asked.

"Barely."

The Nalusa Falaya leapt to the roof on the vault. The first few tentative scratches sounded like fingernails on a chalkboard. Wards or no, I wasn't sure the demon couldn't scratch his way into the vault if he wanted to. I edged out to the portico for a better look, but couldn't see anything without leaving the safety of the crypt. It was too dark to see Lance or the men waiting among the altar stones.

The Muse's song, which sounded incredibly loud inside the vault wasn't loud enough to have much impact on the tree. And with the Muse trapped inside the crypt, there was no way the Nalusa Falaya would be going anywhere near the spirit tree. I had to get the Muse closer to the tree.

CHAPTER 23

I BUZZED LANCE on the walkie-talkie again. "Put your handset in monitor mode and put it on speaker. Then place the set at the foot of the spirit tree. We'll still be able to communicate through Robin's phone. Copy?"

I heard a click of affirmation and then the faint sound of the Muse's song echoed up in stereo from the bottom of the vale.

I grabbed Charlie by the shoulder and shook him. He did not respond. "Enough, with the love songs, Muse. Open the tree."

Charlie's eyes fluttered, but the spirit of the dead girl held him. "Who art thou to command me," she demanded.

As soon as she stopped singing, the demon began to howl. It commenced to scratching on the roof in earnest.

"I am the Hand of Fate, little girl. You open that tree this instant or I will send that creature to the deepest pits of Hell and you will be stuck here alone for eternity with only yourself to blame." I said it with every bit of authority I could muster. I had no idea if she believed me, but she'd attended the white man's church. She'd used the hymnal as a journal. She had to believe in Hell. Ironic that she'd defied her adoptive parents and her clan by taking up with an elemental demon.

Her angry glare surfaced behind Charlie's features—a disturbing sight.

The song began again. Still beautiful, but the yearning quality was gone. Charlie's posture changed— he'd clenched his hands into fists. This was a song of strength—an anthem of sorts.

A loud crack, like a rifle shot reached us from below. Robin checked her phone. "Lance says the tree is opening!"

I used my shears to make a deep cut across Charlie's palm. He didn't even flinch, and the Muse continued her song. I held his dripping hand over the journal, allowing his blood to seep onto the pages of the dead girl's hymnal. Robin gave me a quizzical look, but seemed to understand. She wrapped Charlie's hand in one of the bandages we'd brought with us, while I tucked the book into an inner pocket of my jacket.

"Whatever happens, keep her singing," I said.

"Be careful," Robin answered.

"Of course." I stepped out to the portico and very nearly walked right into the Nalusa Falaya's waiting jaws.

"Give me Muse!" it shouted, its fetid breath choking me with the reek of rotting meat and smoke. Like a great black snake, it writhed across itself restlessly, ever in constant motion. "Give her to me or I will come in there and take her!

Blix appeared beside me, his cell phone on speaker. I turned down the volume. He had maintained the connection to my cell phone, which was inside the crypt. It gave me an idea. The Muse's song faltered, then rang out again, pure and clear. It seemed to agitate the Nalusa Falaya even more.

"You can't," I said. "And you know it." This was the second time the creature had spoken to me. Standing among the columns of the portico, I was outside the wards, yet the creature did not try to attack. Instinctively, I tried to see what was happening down at the spirit tree, but its ever-shifting coils blocked my view. "She's mine. I found her when you could not. I am her master now."

The demon's yellow eyes narrowed—it bared an equally yellow double set of pointy teeth at me. "I don't believe you."

"Believe it or not," I bluffed. "If you want to see her again, you'd best do as I say."

I turned up the volume on Blix's cell phone and took a casual step to the left. The creature's huge head swiveled, its attention focused on me.

"Tch," it sneered. "Bring her to me now or I shall dig you all out like the vermin you are."

From the bottom of the vale, a mule brayed. I couldn't stand it any longer.

I ran like hell down the hill toward the spirit tree.

CHAPTER 24

MUSE'S CLEAR VOICE rang out from Blix's cell phone, as I half-rolled, half-ran down the hill, but the Nalusa Falaya did not give chase. He wasn't fooled—he knew the muse was inside the vault.

I scrambled to my feet and stumbled toward Lance and the lycans. There was a five-foot wide, vertical gash in the trunk, where the outer bark was peeling itself away from its center core. Lance and the three lycans were all up in it, struggling to pull, well, something out of the tree. It didn't look anything like Rhys.

The men were rapidly being overwhelmed by white, luminescent, questing rootlets growing from the base of the tree. The thread-thin strands seemed to be seeking bare patches of skin—especially their hand and faces. Wherever a rootlet touched bare skin, blood flowed from bites inflicted by the blood-sucking mouths at the tip of each glowing nodule. The mule,

Nosey had been spooked by the questing roots, and had managed to stamp and kick at any which approached too closely. It had been Nosey's bray I heard.

My shears were in my hand in an instant. I started at the base of the tree, where the roots were thickest, and proceeded to cut my way through them. Once cut, the brittle roots fell away, and it was almost as if they quickly realized what the shears could do to them, they halted their attack on Lance and the others, and receded back into the base of the tree.

With a great wrenching pull, the man-sized lump of stiffened tissue was pulled free of the central core of the tree, into the waiting arms of Lance and Roland.

I hovered anxiously as they laid Rhys out on the travois. "What's wrong with him?"

"We've got him, Mattie," Lance said. "Get out of the way and let us get him out of here."

Rhys was unconscious—still as death. His stiff body was as twisted and desiccated as road kill. His skin was hard—like wood. I pulled my hand away, as if burned, but I knew for certain he was in there. I felt for a heart beat—a single lub.

"He's alive!" Somehow, impossibly, but alive. Already, the tree was folding over itself, closing up.

A sudden scream rang out from the crypt, snapping me out of my reverie. Robin's voice shouted through the phone. "He's coming!"

I scooped up the walkie-talkie handset without

thinking, adrenaline pumping. "Get out of here, guys. I've got this." I ran forward a few paces into the clearing to meet the monster face on.

"What the hell, Matt," Lance protested.

"Go, go, go," I urged. "Get out of here! I know what I'm doing." The drumming beat in my head was back. Rhys was safe. There was nothing left to do but get the Nalusa Falaya back in the tree.

The Nalusa Falaya flowed toward me its body a pulsating fog that obliterated the snowy landscape beneath it.

The drumming in my head faltered. I got the distinct feeling that this time, it meant business.

Cripes. That little ghost bitch had sent her demon lover after me.

CHAPTER 25

THE SMOKE DEMON reshaped itself and a shadowy man appeared, outlined from within by the glow of will-o-the-wisps. Less solid than when he was up at the crypt, but more defined. Bare-chested, he wore leather leggings and a tall, Abe-Lincoln-type hat. The creature steepled its long fingers, tapping three inch-long talons together with a clacking sound that sent goose-bumps up my spine. His feet left no prints on the snow.

I held my ground; waiting until I could no longer hear the receding footfalls of men or the jingling of Nosey's harness. Blix hovered near the spirit tree, but I waved him away. If I was right about this, the roots of the spirit tree were attracted to souls. The Nalusa Falaya carried the souls of his victims inside him. The smoke demon would be irresistible to the tree, but only if I could bring it within reach of the pale questing roots.

I backed myself up against the base of the trunk.

Immediately, the roots of the tree crawled over my boots and began climbing up my legs. The walkie-talkie set was still in monitor mode. The muse would be able to hear every word I said.

The Nalusa Falaya loomed before me. Close, but not close enough.

"I'm glad you're here, I said, my voice as steady as I could make it. I shifted my feet, trying to prevent the rootlets from getting a good grip on me. They were fragile, but there were a lot of them. They were attracted to blood; mine, if they could get it, but more than that, the spirit tree wanted the blood of its creators, the Senequois.

Just like the Nalusa Falaya.

They were meant for each other.

I pulled the journal soaked in Charlie's blood from beneath my jacket and held it up before me.

"This is what you want, isn't it," I cooed.

The demon's nostrils flared at the scent of fresh blood. Blue sparks flashed behind the black pits where his eyes might have been. The creature stretched its open maw wide—multiple rows of razor-keen shark teeth gleamed wetly. Backed up against the gaping tree trunk, I had nowhere to go. The demon's noxious breath turned my stomach.

"Give it to me," he said.

"It was never her," I shouted, holding up the book.

"You played with her because she amused you. You wanted her blood, but they killed her and trapped her soul where you can't get to it. The Muse is no good to you now. Only the blood and souls of the People can satisfy your thirst for revenge."

The singing stopped. A moment later, Robin yelled at me from inside the crypt, "You better get up here, Mattie. Something's happening."

I wrenched my leg away from the network of roots, and nearly lost my footing. I held the bloody book against the hollow crack in the spirit tree. The trunk vibrated, as if from some great inner stress.

"You can smell it, can't you? I've got the blood of the People right here. Only I can give you what you really want."

The Nalusa Falaya seemed to go all smoky for a minute, and reached for the book. I snatched it away, holding the ancient hymnal inside the ever-closing hollow of the spirit tree. The Nalusa Falaya wasn't solid enough in this form to wrest the book away from me.

The roots wrapped around my legs seemed to sense that bigger prey was afoot and released their grip. My legs and feet were no longer bound. Instead, they groped my arm blindly, reaching for the blood-stained book.

"Nooooo," the Muse's voice sang out across the vale.

"Mattie!" Robin sounded desperate. "It's Charlie!"

Oh cripes, not Charlie!

"Give it to me," the demon hissed. The will-o-the-wisps inside him buzzed like hornets, further dissipating his smoky form.

"Knock yourself out, Ashface." With a flick of my wrist, I dropped the Muse's diary into the chasm at the center of the spirit tree.

Like a swarm of angry bees, the Nalusa Falaya dissolved into the shape of a funnel cloud, and streamed into the tree. A few quick cuts with my shears, and my hand was free of the thready roots. Thousands of questing rootlets reached for individual particles of smoke, drawing them deeper into the tree. With a groan, the crack in the tree began to close. A few wisps of smoke tried to escape, but all were captured and sucked inside the tree.

The Muse's song, like a lullaby, continued to echo out across the vale. As the fissure in the tree grew smaller, I threw the handset inside it. A trilled note, long and low and achingly beautiful, warbled out of the walkie-talkie until the spirit tree twisted itself shut, abruptly cutting off the sound of her voice.

I raced back up the trail toward the vault as fast as I could.

"Charlie!" In the dim lamplight, Charlie lay on the marble floor of the vault, his body clenched, as if in pain, his head cradled in Robin's lap.

"I don't know what to do," she said, her expression pained.

The old man's eyes held mine, but when he tried to speak, it was the Muse's voice I heard.

"You lied to me," she hissed. "You took him from me and you lied to me. Now I will take this one. I know you love him."

Her threat tore at me.

"Get out of him," I ordered. I grabbed Charlie's injured hand and gripped it hard within my own. He winced, but her image still hovered beneath his skin. "You have no power here."

She laughed. Slowly, as if against his will, Charlie pushed himself to a seated position. "Maybe I'll keep him here with me."

I scrambled to my feet. "Come on, Robin, Help me drag him outside. She won't be able to cross the portal. She'll be forced to leave his body."

Robin gave me a worried look. "I don't think that's a good idea."

"I will stop his heart if you try," the Muse promised. "I can do that. Or, I can drive him mad. I can do both. He's mine now."

Charlie made a high keening sound.

Doh! "Leave him alone!" There had to be a way--.

Blix flew into the crypt and immediately hissed at Charlie, something he'd never done before. It gave me an idea.

"Annie!" I shouted. "I summon you."

In seconds, Annie's leathery wings buffeted the top of the vault as she circled once before she settled down beside Charlie. As soon as she landed, she began to growl and snap her jaws together in agitation. I knelt beside her, lest she try to dig the ghost from her master's body with her fearsome sharp claws.

"Easy, girl," I cautioned.

"He is hurt," she said, in her soft, child-like voice. Annie sounds a little like Miss Piggy. "Possessed."

"Yes," I agreed. Charlie's eyes had closed. His breathing had become erratic. "He needs your help. Will you sing to him?"

Annie cocked her head at me. "What shall I sing?"

I looked at Robin, who nodded. "His favorite," we both said.

Immediately, the pterodactyl-form djemon began to sing *Twinkle Twinkle Little Star*. The simple tune, sung like a whispered lullaby, brought about an immediate reaction from the Muse.

"Stop that!" The muse's transparent arms left Charlie's body to put her hands on Charlie's ears. "Stop that wretched yowling!"

But it wasn't wretched at all. It was charming and sweet and solemn. And the animated way in which Annie sang it, with her long claw-tipped fingers clasped together, as if in prayer, while she bobbed her bullet-shaped head to the beat, had Robin and I singing along and clapping for the chorus. I had no idea there were so many verses. The Muse emerged from Charlie's body half-way through the third chorus and sulked into the furthest corner of the ceiling.

No one felt the least bit sorry for her.

Charlie opened his own eyes and the four of us sang the final chorus together. Annie preened with pleasure as the old medicine man sat up and thanked her for singing such a fine song. He gave me a wink. "Best singin' I heard all night."

Annie spotted the bloody handkerchief wrapped around his hand. He unwrapped the fabric and showed her the wound, which she examined as carefully as any nurse. Already, the wound had stopped bleeding, and begun to heal. "Tell me, Girlie," he said. "How did it go?"

"Not like we expected." I answered. "You were right about using your blood to lure the demon to the tree. I didn't want to cut you, but there was no other way. And the closer it got to the tree, the more difficult it became for the Nalusa Falaya to maintain its physical form."

Charlie held out his hand for Annie to inspect. "It's the blood of The People, Mattie. Their sacrifice created the tree. As long as their souls remain trapped within the immortal Nalusa Falaya, the two are bound by an unbreakable link. In its weakened state, the demon will never again be able to escape and deliver its revenge."

Charlie flexed his fingers. "Where's Rhys? Did you get him?"

I glanced at Robin. "He's out, but that's all we know."

From the woods on the opposite side of the vale, a mule brayed.

"Well, come on, then, Girlie. I'm about to freeze my keester off. Let's get out of here."

CHAPTER 26

MY HONDA WAS already gone when we got back to the parking lot. So were Roland and Luke's trucks. Terry's brother Neil helped get Adelaide loaded into the horse trailer. The brothers had agreed to give Charlie a ride home, so as soon as Charlie was settled inside their truck, I thanked them for the hundredth time and headed home as fast as I dared with an exhausted Robin riding behind me on the Vic.

I found Lance kneeling next to Rhys, who was stretched out on the floor of the parlor, stiff as a board. The whole house reeked of pine tar and road kill.

I dropped to my knees beside Rhys and kissed him. Immediately, I pulled away, as if burned. My lips began to sting. "What happened?" Rhys's eyes were closed. "Has he said anything?"

"I thought we'd have to chop him out," Lance explained. "But after the first few cuts, the tree sort of pulled away from around him. What happened with the demon?"

A roaring sound filled my ears. My lips had gone numb. I couldn't speak. Dimly, I heard Robin tell Lance what happened.

I touched my fingers to my mouth. Charlie said the tree was poison. Maybe it had poisoned. Rhys, too. Looking at him now, I could not imagine that this twisted knot of human jerky was the man I'd given my heart to. His skin had the look and texture of dried leather. His face and body had lost every shred of fat. His beard had grown—and turned the same lichen grey-brown color as the rest of his body, drained of color by the pervasive woody pulp of the tree's inner core. Even his expression, frozen in an agonized grimace, carried woody pulp in every crease. Another week or two, and he would have been encased within a solid wood cocoon. He wasn't breathing. Only the slow lub of his heart gave any indication that he was alive at all.

Relief and guilt warred within me. How long had he suffered before losing consciousness? I hated that I'd lost count of the days between All Hallows Eve and tonight—Winter Solstice. Longest night of the year, in more ways than one.

"What do you want to do with him?" Lance asked.

Rhys wasn't human—no doctor could tell us what to do. I doubted whether anyone on the planet, much less in Shore Haven had any kind of experience with this kind of healing.

I gave Robin a pleading look.

"I'm not a healer, I'm sorry."

"Help me get him upstairs and into the tub," I said. It was all I could think of. Maybe a soak in warm water would revive him, or at least start to rehydrate him.

After getting him into the tub of warm water, Lance and Robin went off to bed. I sat beside the tub, adding hot water, whenever necessary. I couldn't tell if he could hear me, but I spoke to him for a long time, until I fell asleep with my chin on the edge of the tub.

By morning, his body was no longer stiff was a board, but rested naturally in the bottom of the tub. His joints moved when I flexed them, and his expression had softened. Better, but still unconscious, with a sickly grey pallor.

Sometime later, Lance stuck his head in. "Robin needs to get back to Toronto," he said. "I'm going with her."

I must've been drowsing. I blinked in the wan light of the winter sun streaming through the voile curtains of the bathroom window. If Rhys looked like road kill, Lance looked half-past dead. We both knew his luck had turned—I could see it on him. He *had* to leave. "When?"

"I'm bringing Robin over to meet Mina this afternoon." He shrugged. Until he met Robin, Mina was the only person Lance ever truly cared about. "We'll hit road right after."

"How long will you be gone?"

"I don't know." He touched my cheek. "It's better this way, Matt. For both of us."

I nodded. "Look, I've got some things I have to take care of. I need a couple hours. Will you stay with Rhys until I get back?"

"It'll take me that long to pack the car."

When I stepped off the elevator at the Sheriff's office, the remains of a celebration was clearly in evidence. The last few slices of chocolate cake sat in paper plates next to a large coffee urn.

Somebody's birthday, I figured, but I was wrong.

"It's about time you showed up." Sheriff Reynolds' voice boomed from his office. "Grab yourself a piece of cake and get in here, Blackman."

Hard to tell if he was pleased or angry. I had no time for cake.

The FBI special investigator, Hugo Green, was seated in the one of the guest chairs across from the Sheriff. Both men looked like something the cat dragged in. I'd never seen Green without a tie. Or a jacket, for that matter.

I wasn't keen on talking to Jimbo in front of the

FBI. I stood on the doorway. "What's up?"

"I just got the call." Agent Green patted his cell phone. "The truck arrived twenty minutes ago."

"What truck?"

"Check your messages, Blackman." Sheriff Reynolds said, without rancor. "The truck carrying the vat of liquid nitrogen. John Fewkes, the leader of the Penfield Witch Cult and two of his followers are now part of the permanent popsicle collection at Quantico."

"You got him?"

Both men chuckled.

"Don't look so surprised, Deputy," Agent Green said. "The FBI knows how to deal with demon masters—or just about any other supernatural predator you can imagine."

Not even Blix had seen the takedown. "How did you catch him?"

Green explained. "We set it up in a warehouse, not far from the cult headquarters. Told him we had the book. A swap deal for our kidnapped man, Cusick. The sorcerer was leery, but we agreed to his conditions—he wanted us to prop open all the doors and windows."

"We didn't understand why until he showed up in Raven form," Jimbo offered. "We had our best sharpshooter hidden in the rafters, but hitting a bird is a lot harder than hitting a man. I honestly thought we'd blown it."

The two lawmen exchanged a weighty glance. "The

sniper was smart—he took his time. He waited until Fewkes circled the inside of the warehouse a couple of times," Reynolds explained. "When he swooped down to pick up the book, the sniper hit him with a mega-load of ketamine. He dropped like a stone."

"He never had a chance to call up that smoke demon of his," Agent Green noted. "We had a liquid nitrogen tanker truck standing by, two blocks away. Once he was down, we moved in. We had him in the tank in minutes."

The sheriff made a placating gesture. "Maybe not quite that easy. A couple of his cultist buddies showed up and tried to interfere, but we got him, and that's all that matters. John Fewkes is no more."

Maybe Maestro hadn't shown up after all. "But he's immortal."

"Doesn't matter." Green looked grim. "That vat of liquid nitrogen will be buried miles beneath the earth, where no one will ever be able to reach him."

"That's the beauty of it," Jimbo interrupted. "John Fewkes is a terrorist. His property and valuables have been seized by the government and will be sold at auction, with part of the proceeds going to maintaining his Cryo care. Everything else will be divided among his victims."

The reminder of what could happen to me if anyone found out about Blix chilled me, even as I bathed in the glow of the lawmen's celebration. "You mean like

Honey Briscoe and her kids?"

Agent Green nodded. "Mrs. Briscoe and the other victims will be able to apply for compensation, although we haven't done a financial audit yet. I'm not certain what kind of resources Fewkes had. It'll take a while for the courts to decide."

Sheriff Reynolds gave me a thoughtful look. "How did your stakeout go last night?"

Jim Reynolds is so much smarter than anyone gives him credit for. I'd told him we were going to try to keep the Nalusa Falaya distracted while the team went after Fewkes. "The usual. Broke a curse. Banished a demon. Freed a genie."

Green stared at me for a beat, and even Jimbo gave me a wary look. "You banished a demon?"

"Just kidding." I said. "The suspect never showed. It was a late night." I yawned hugely. "I was hoping I could get a couple days off."

That Jimbo didn't know what to believe gave me a weird little sense of satisfaction.

"Sorry Blackman, no can do. Everybody wants to take holidays at Christmas, and I'm not going to make an exception. Wolf Patrol doesn't get special favors."

I wasn't surprised.

A light sleet made the roads icy coming home.

Robin's Volkswagen Passat was loaded to the max with Lance's tools and clothes. He wasn't planning to come back this way anytime soon. It didn't take a psychic to see that they were together—and that they belonged together.

"Charlie sent Terry over with a package of herbs and stuff, with instructions on how to cook it up as a poultice to draw the poison out of Rhys," Robin said.

Lance patted his chest. "I took a little for myself, but the rest of it is on the stove, cooling."

He still looked tired, but his lifeline glowed more strongly than when he'd first arrived. Maybe it was Robin's steadying influence, or that they were going to see his daughter, Mina. He appeared more grounded—more like his old self. Or maybe, Charlie's herbal concoction had something to do with it. For Rhys's sake, I hoped so.

"Take care, Matt." Lance kissed my forehead. "The new job suits you—a whole lot better than that meter maid gig. Congratulations, Deputy. You've found your groove. Guess you don't need me anymore."

I grinned up at him. "That doesn't mean I don't want you in my life, you big stupid grease monkey."

"Love you too, brat. Keep in touch."

"I'm not the one who always leaves and never calls." I complained, more sharply than I intended.

Robin hugged me and gave me her contact information. She smelled of fresh-mown grass. "We'll be back this summer, if not before."

Yes. I could see it. A picnic by the lake with Mina. A trip to the Sterling Renaissance Festival.

"You know I'll be back," he joked, his smile easy. "You're the only one who can read my future."

"Drive safe," I said, because I didn't want them to leave at all.

Rhys lay on my bed, a couple of old quilts tucked in around him. I felt his forehead, which was cool to the touch. Every time I touched his bare skin, my own skin reddened and burned. The toxic smell of him filled the room. The pulse at his neck beat far too slow to be believed.

Still not breathing.

I brought the pot full of boiled herbs and leaves upstairs. The poultice mixture was a thick coarse paste, dark green in color. Thick enough that I used a wooden spoon to scoop out fist-sized portion of it. The goop had an astringent scent which seemed to mitigate the ghastly scent of foul poison in Rhys's body. Charlie's instructions said to smear it across his torso and then wrap it in place with clean cloth bandages to hold it against his skin.

The stuff was as thick as peanut butter. I put on rubber gloves and used my hands to slather it on.

Almost immediately, the stiffness in Rhys's limbs and torso began to ease. By the time I was finished bandaging him, Rhys's frozen expression of anguish had smoothed to one of peace.

I was encouraged by that more than anything.

For the next three days, I cooked up Charlie's poultice recipe every day and re-applied the mash as instructed, twice a day. Rhys no longer looked like petrified jerky. He was still unconscious though, and had not yet drawn a breath.

I hated leaving Rhys alone while I was at work, and felt terribly guilty every time I left the house, but wolf patrol was the only thing that could distract me from the hopelessness I felt every time I looked at Rhys.

"It's not working," I told Charlie. "He's not breathing." It was Christmas Eve, and I'd stopped in at Charlie's with a Wegmans turkey dinner for two with all the trimmings before I started my shift. I poured gravy over the mashed potatoes and turkey on my plate.

Charlie had far more faith in his medicine than I did. "Look at your hand, Girlie. It sucked that dreamspider poison right out of you."

I hadn't even noticed. "Good heavens," I marveled. The black venom stain left by Felicity Caprice's spider bite was gone. My once-blackened left hand was now the same color as my right. "You're right." I wiggled my fingers. *Cool.*

"So how much longer is this going to take? I thought djenies were supposed to heal fast. Why won't he wake up?"

"He'll come around," Charlie assured me. "He is aware."

After three days of tending to Rhys, my sinuses had shut down. I couldn't even smell my food. Sheesh. "I'm not much good at this nursemaid stuff. What if I'm doing it wrong?"

Charlie took a bite of yam topped with cranberry sauce and hummed appreciatively. With the faux fire going in his electric fireplace and Annie curled up in her bed in the corner, Charlie's cabin felt more homey and festive than the big old Queen Anne where I was supposed to be taking care of Rhys.

"Patience." He scanned the table. "Is there pie?"

"Of course. It wouldn't be Christmas dinner without pie."

"Bring it over then, Girlie. No need to wait for dessert. I'll be too full to eat it by then."

I grinned and got up to get the pie. "You're a man after my own heart, Charlie."

Dinner with Charlie reminded me how badly the warring odors of tree poison and healing poultice herbs had messed up my sinuses. I still had the little brown bottle of sweet orange oil Rhys had given me when I'd suffered terribly from teratosis. One drop of that stuff had completely rebooted my sinuses. It seemed so long ago.

The bottle had been sitting at the back of the bathroom medicine cabinet for months.

I unstoppered the rubber seal and touched my fingertip to the dropper inside. I remembered how Rhys tilted my head back and anointed the center of my forehead. Your third eye, he'd told me. Clear your thoughts.

This time, the clearing of my sinuses wasn't nearly as arousing as when Rhys had done it, but I felt refreshed and clear-headed. The first thing I noticed was that house didn't smell like poison tree or poultice much at all—only the scent of toothpaste lingered in the bathroom. It was my memory of that scent which lingered—it wasn't real.

I went into my bedroom, where Rhys lay still as a corpse. The smell had been so bad; I'd taken to sleeping on the sofa downstairs. Now, the room was just a room. It no longer smelled bad.

I turned on the lamp next to the bed. Rhys's complexion no longer looked ashen. His beard had darkened. There were still streaks of lichen-colored hair running through it, but his skin was unlined except for the corners of his eyes. Charlie was right— Rhys was improving. He'd look far younger without the beard—another stab of guilt. I should have shaved him, at least.

"I'm so sorry," I said, for the millionth time. Maybe this would work. Then again, maybe it wouldn't.

"Clear your thoughts," I whispered, and dabbed a drop of orange oil on the pad of my thumb. I held it to the center of his forehead, and then massaged the oil into his skin in a circular motion.

He gasped.

I jumped.

He opened his eyes—cloudy and blind as the eyes of a long-dead fish.

A sob tore through me. The spirit tree had destroyed Rhys Warrick.

He grabbed my wrist in an iron grip and pulled me close. A hiss-like growl escaped his lips.

It sounded like a question. "What did you say?"

"How long?" His voice sounded like two boulders grinding together. He took another breath. "Inside?"

He blinked rapidly, and put his hands to his eyes, removing the now-cloudy green contact lenses he always wore. His eyes glowed with the unnatural yellow gleam of a djenie in full control of his senses.

It was Rhys.

I burst into tears. "You're alive!" I stooped to kiss him, but he pushed me away.

"What's wrong?"

He struggled to get up, managing only to brace

himself on one elbow. "Mattie, this is important." The effort to speak seemed to take enormous effort. "How long was I in the tree?"

What? I frowned. This was not going the way I thought would. "Fifty-two days. Everyone thought you were dead." *I thought you were dead.*

He grimaced and threw off his covers, before trying to get up again. He was so thin. This time, he managed to swing his feet to the floor, but standing was beyond his capability. I tried to push him back down. "Wait! You almost died," I said."

As wretched as he looked, he was stronger than me.

"No," he panted. He got a grip on the bed's iron headboard and used it to brace himself as he managed to stand. "I've been a druid for six centuries. This isn't my first rodeo."

Naked except for the poultice-soaked bandages wrapped around his chest, he shuffled down the hall like an old man, using the wall to brace himself.

"Let me help you, Rhys." I grabbed his arm.

He froze. "Don't." He said it quietly, but firmly.

I let go, burned by the tone of his voice. "What's wrong?"

He turned to look at me, and then looked away. "You did the right thing by rehydrating me in the tub, and I thank you, but I'm full of poison. You've got to keep your distance. I'm toxic as hell. I've got to get out of here."

"What—no! The poultice sucked it all out of you. The poison is gone."

He reached the bathroom. Already his movements seemed less labored. "The Nalusa Falaya," he said. He wouldn't look at me. "Where is it?"

"It's back in the tree."

He seemed to relax a little. "Good. Spirit tree poison works from the inside out, eating its prisoner at a cellular level. The reason the Nalusa Falaya appeared smoke-like at times is because it had lost its ability to retain a solid shape. After three hundred years, even an immortal demon loses substance. Eventually, the victim becomes fully absorbed by the tree."

"But you're okay, right? Charlie said the poultice sucked all the venom out..."

He wiped a milky smear of sweat from his brow and rubbed it between his fingers. "The poultice got some of it, but the rest of it is down deep. The only way to get it out is to sweat it out." He licked his cracked, dry lips. He gave me a brief glance, then looked away. "Get me some clothes, will you? I'm going to Master Foo's."

The silence stretched between us. "For how long?" My voice cracked.

He wouldn't look at me. "As a druid, I've been imprisoned in a tree on two other occasions—neither tree was toxic, but coming back from those ordeals wasn't easy." He patted his bandaged chest. "The worst of the poison is down deep, understand? Until I get it out, I'm lethal. I can't be around you—or any human—while I'm like this."

My stomach lurched. "You're serious." He sounded so calm about this. I swallowed the awful certainty that if he left, I'd never see him again. "I don't want you to go." I hated the pleading in my voice.

"One of the things I admire most about you is your independence, Mattie. Human life is too short to waste. Don't wait on me."

And with that, he stepped into the bathroom and locked the door behind him.

I stared at the closed door for a long moment, trying to decide what to do. Rhys had always been so strong. So certain. Now he was acting like—I don't know. Like he didn't even know me. What the hell, Rhys?

Thirty minutes later, I watched him shamble down the sidewalk in Henri's pea coat and jeans, hunched up against the sleet. He even refused to let me go with him.

"No need. I can manage on my own," he said.

CHAPTER 27

TWO WEEKS LATER, Honey Bee's Bakery reopened.

Of course I'd heard about it through the law enforcement grapevine, but I waited a week, until some of the furor died down. Needless to say, Honey's muffins and donuts had been sorely missed by every law enforcement officer on the day shift.

I stopped in just before closing on Saturday afternoon, hoping she'd have time to catch up.

"Oh Mattie, it's so good to see you!" Honey came around the counter and gave me a big hug. "I hoped you'd stop by today." In spite of the ordeal she and her two sons had been through, she looked younger and happier than I'd seen her in a long time.

"They let me be there for John Fewkes capture," she confessed. "I didn't think they'd go for it, but Sheriff Reynolds stood up for me. They'd rigged the warehouse with hidden cameras and microphones. I was able to watch the whole thing on from the support van, parked a block away." She shook her head. "Although it was pretty touch and go for a while."

"You were there? They told me it went off without a hitch. A perfect setup."

She rolled her eyes. "Oh the setup was perfect, but that was the only thing that went right. The sniper hit the sorcerer with two ketamine darts, but they had no effect. He changed into human form, grabbed the book, and started throwing fireballs at the sniper, who was hiding up in the rafters. The sniper was trapped. Agents swarmed the building, but Fewkes threw more fireballs at them and the Feds were forced to back off."

She leaned forward confidentially. "Then, from out of nowhere, a guy in a tuxedo, top hat, and spats, stepped out of the shadows and walks toward Fewkes. He had his arms spread wide, as if to show he had no weapons. He's got a big ol' smile on his face, but he's not saying anything. Fewkes freaks out and starts screaming at him. He knocks him back with some kind of invisible blast. It blew his hat off, but the guy kept coming. Then Fewkes sort of collapsed—he falls to his knees. He's still spitting mad, but in less than a minute, he was unconscious. The guy seemed to know all about the cameras. He waved the Feds in to help the sniper and get Fewkes. He knew all about the truck of liquid nitrogen they had waiting, and told them that they had less than ten minutes to get him immersed into tank. Then he thanked them for dinner and wished them a pleasant evening."

"Great stars." Maestro and Stella had come through after all. "Dinner, huh?"

"Yes. The microphones picked up every word. The cameras flickered for several seconds, so the guy didn't show up on film. The engineers called it a power surge. I don't know what he did, but without that man, Fewkes would have gotten away. I got the feeling he wasn't alone, either. Just before he disappeared, he said 'Let's go.' Anyway, John Fewkes, the man who killed my husband and grandmother is gone. I will never have to testify against him in court. He will never be free. That's a huge weight lifted off my life. Whatever we had to go was worth it, although I miss Lou something terrible."

"I miss him too." I told her about Lou setting me up to take over wolf patrol with the Sheriff's Office.

"I know," she said. "I spoke to Charlie last week. He told me about Rhys." Her eyes met mine. "How is he?"

I swallowed the sudden lump in my throat. I couldn't even begin to describe it. "He's different. Like he doesn't remember—or want to remember—us. He spends all day training with Master Foo, and then goes back to his place to sleep. The only time I see him now is at Qhua Bei practice with Master Foo."

I'd been going every day.

Physically, Rhys looked as good to me as he ever did. Better, even. He'd shaved off his hair, and it was growing in shiny black. The fu-Manchu moustache was back. His muscle tone and definition had returned. His skin had regained that healthy, warm brown color I found myself dreaming about.

"You seem different, too," she said.

"I guess I am," I admitted. Working out every day hadn't hurt me any, either. I'd improved so much that Master Foo had given me a real blade, a smaller version of the one Rhys used. My daily practice, combined with my growing confidence in my abilities on wolf patrol had made me harder, leaner. Sheriff Reynolds told me he he'd noticed a difference in how I carried myself. There wasn't a lycan in town that could intimidate me.

"Maybe Master Foo can help."

I rolled my eyes. "Master Foo isn't exactly interested in matters of the heart." Although, I had to admit, I'd felt Rhys's gaze linger on me a couple of times; usually after practice, when my hair was soaked with sweat, and my arms covered with bruises and welts. Our blade edges were blunt, but even a dull blade could draw blood. Or maybe I just imagined it. I had a sneaking suspicion that it was the sparring that roused Rhys, not me. "I don't think--."

"What?"

I couldn't say it. The idea that Rhys and I might not

get back together hurt too much to even think about. "Chief Halliday asked me out. On a date."

"I hear he's the new Alpha of the Penfield pack," Honey sounded carefully neutral.

"I didn't say yes." Well, not exactly. But a little thrill shot through me when he asked. "I told him I'd think about it." And every time I did, I felt guilty.

"Rhys will come around, Mattie. Listen, I wanted ask you about something, but I don't want it to get out just yet." She went to the front door, locked it, and flipped the sign to "Closed." At the cash register, she took a check out from beneath the cash drawer. "I received this in the mail yesterday." She slid it across the table toward me. "It's an offer to buy me out."

I whistled. "Wow. That's a lot of zeroes."

"It's a fair offer," she said. "Look at the signature."

Otto Russ.

My stomach squelched uncomfortably. The richest guy in Shore Haven. The man responsible for launching the town's new Marina project. Otto's father, Obart, had practically founded Germantown and Shore Haven; the family still owned most of the commercial real estate in the area.

Rhys and Blix were the only living beings besides me who knew the awful truth—that 'Mad' Otto Russ was the firstborn son of my great-grandmother, Madame Coumlie and Obart Russ, the man who kidnapped, raped and enslaved her for years—a tradition of abuse that was perpetuated by Otto as soon as he was old enough.

Garland Russ, Otto's only child by marriage, as much as admitted that he was my father out of wedlock. I'd never met the man, but billionaire Mad Otto Russ was many things—including a known demon master. And through rape and incest, my grandfather three times over.

"I heard he was in a coma. How is that even possible?" Mad Otto was supposed to be confined to bed, with a machine doing the work that his heart and lungs weren't able to. The sheriff told me it was the only reason he hadn't been arrested.

"I'm sure he has people to handle the business side of things," she answered.

"Why would he offer to buy you out?" I asked.

"This isn't the first time he's made an offer," she said, softly. "But he's never sent a check before—at least not to me. He owns all the property slated for the new marina, and over the past few years, he's bought up about half the properties along Third Street."

Bunny Tacker had said as much, when she told me her parents her parents had sold their shoe store.

"There are a few of us," she continued, "Who don't want to sell. And yet, over time, one way or another, the property always ends up in his hands. The last three or four people who refused to sell are gone. Margie Foyle, who owned the Tog Shop, sold out three years ago.

She left town and was never heard from again—even though her daughter still lives in Picston. Two years ago, Coil and Spring Watch Repair was foreclosed on by Otto's bank, Germantown Savings and Loan. Last year, it was Killer Dave's."

I gave her a sharp look. "Mel Moody did not sell Killer Dave's. He was murdered." By either Felicity Caprice or her Dreamspider boyfriend, Luçien Bold.

"His heirs didn't want the restaurant. Otto made them an offer." She slipped the check into the pocket of her apron. "In the end, Otto got what he wanted. Mel's refusal to sell Killer Dave's was the last thing standing between Otto and owning the entire block. The planning commission approved Otto's plans for a high rise luxury hotel there last week. Construction of the new marina starts this spring."

"I don't believe that Mad Otto arranged to have Mel Moody killed."

"I don't want to sell, but when Felicity sold Les Belles Jolie and moved to Arizona so sudden, I think I became the next in line."

"Felicity didn't--" I stopped. Local gossip said Felicity Caprice had moved to Arizona to be closer to her kids. Ugh. It sounded a whole lot better than the truth, which was that she had been the dreamspider brood mother who'd bitten me. Now that I thought about it, there were a lot more businesses closing down than could be explained as normal. Bunny

Tacker told me it was her mother's fall on the ice and broken hip that had convinced her parents to close their shoe store. Shanghai Palace had been shut down by the health department weeks ago. It should have re-opened by now. Rhys had moved back to his apartment over Mystic Properties. He didn't own the place—it was a lease, but...

Honey waved her hand in front of my face. "Are you okay?"

I blushed. "Yeah, sorry, go on," I said. Whatever thought I'd been reaching for was gone. Focus, Mattie. "I'm listening."

"I said that after all this John Fewkes cult business was over, I thought I'd be able to raise my boys in peace, and get on with life." She gave me a sad little smile. "You know Charlie has offered to tutor Arby in the old ways—teach him the language; train him as a shaman. Arby is over the moon about it. And the Rochester Rhinos have invited Nate to attend the Junior Rhinos tryouts this summer."

"Wow, that is a big deal." The schools never offered summer soccer—they said it was too hot for the kids.

Holy crap.

I felt as if I'd been smacked upside the head by Morta herself. I don't know why I hadn't seen it before. Why had the dreamspiders come to Shore Haven in the first place? Abe Lightner told me dreamspiders couldn't survive in cold weather. They craved the heat. They would never have survived the winter in upstate New York. Who could have convinced Luçien Bold to come to Shore Haven? Someone with a lot of money. Otto Russ? Maybe. But why? There had to be a reason. A compulsion of certainty swept through me like a dry desert wind. The cards would show me the connections.

"You know what the boys and I have been through, Mattie. If I take this check, I'll have a stake to start over somewhere else. Besides, with the new marina and the fancy hotel and theatre going in, Shore Haven won't be the kind of quiet, quaint little town I want to raise my kids in anymore." She stared out the window, blinking away sudden tears. "I don't want to go. I feel connected to this place. This is the land of my history, my People. We have always lived here. The air is cleaner here—the water is sweeter." She sighed. "I'm tired of fighting. I want my boys to be safe."

Worry hovered around her like a vapor. "I don't want you to go, either. When will you decide?"

She sighed. "The check is payable for sixty days. I hate moving the boys during the school year, but I have to put their safety first. If I turn down his offer, I won't feel safe."

Taking Mad Otto's money wouldn't make her safe. Not even close. I didn't want to scare her, but I had an idea—not a plan yet, but something. I gripped her hand. "Don't sign anything yet."

CHAPTER 28

I PARKED IN the lot behind Mystic Properties and waited for Rhys to arrive. I reasoned that he wouldn't see my car until he turned into the lot, and hoped he wouldn't decide to drive off. I flipped through the pages in the manila folder Blix had printed out for me, silently rehearsing my speech over and over. Blix had his usual brilliant job with the data—but I needed someone I trusted to look at it objectively. Selfishly, I suppose I just wanted to talk to Rhys alone.

I heard the rumble of his truck before his headlights lit up the Honda's interior. There was a slight hesitation, and then Rhys pulled the pickup into the spot next to my car. I got out and walked around the truck to greet him, my heart in my throat.

He got out of the truck, and stood there, in the dark.

"It's me," I said. I clasped the folder to my chest,

my fingers fidgeting with the corners.

"I see that."

Amused or irritated? I couldn't tell. "I need your help," I said, my teeth chattering. Dang, it was cold out.

"I don't think I'm up to it. I've been a bit under the weather lately," he said, not unkindly.

"What? No, not that!" The blush heated me down to my toes. "I mean, I know. Wait. I came here to talk to you. I want you to take me into the caves beneath Sentinel Hill."

His surprise lasted a long beat. "Well, since you put it that way, how can I say no? Come on in before we both freeze."

Amusement, then. My heart unclenched a little.

But instead of leading me up the stairs to his apartment, he switched on the office lights downstairs and motioned me to take a seat on the old grey sofa in the back of the store. A little disappointing, but okay.

I couldn't wait any longer. Over the next hour, I laid out my theory to him, piece by piece, property by property, year by year. Obituary by obituary.

Rhys paced the room like a panther; nodding but not saying much until I was finished. Then he powered up his computer and I watched over his shoulder as he cross-checked the public records that Blix had discovered with the online county archives and newspaper reports.

"I think you're right. It does look a long con. A guy that age, though--."

My cell phone rang. The call was for a lycan domestic disturbance in Henrietta. "I've got to go," I said. "What do you think?"

The look he gave me made my thighs tremble. "I'm in," was all he said. "Come back when you're done and we'll figure out the rest of it together."

On Valentine's Day, heavy banks of snow-laden clouds began drifting over Lake Ontario. The blizzard was expected to hit after midnight, but the streets of Shore Haven had all but emptied hours before. The only activity in Germantown was the slow stream of traffic into the parking lot at Maestro's Dance Studio.

A massive white tent and awning sheltered the red carpet that had been set up so that guests could arrive in style. Sharp-eyed parking attendants hustled to keep the traffic moving. Across the street, Rhys and I slumped side-by-side in the toasty-warm cab of Rhys's truck, watching the arrival of guests through binoculars.

When Rhys and I laid out our plan to Hugo Green, he'd loved it, except for the location. "Too many civilians can get hurt. We've got to stop him before he gets inside the building." He was right. We didn't need to catch all the fish in one net, but we wouldn't have another chance at catching the biggest one.

I had a hard time concentrating on the cars. I mean, I can appreciate the lean lines of a Ferrari or Lotus as much as the next girl, but our target would be making a very different sort of statement.

And the sight of Rhys in a tuxedo had just about taken my breath away. Sitting next to him with my leg jammed next to his had my motor purring overtime.

"There it is," Rhys said. The maroon Duisenberg rolled past us, as elegant as a luxury yacht. "Nice."

"Supercharged," I agreed.

"We've got it," Green's voice whispered in my ear piece. Green didn't need a warrant to arrest a demon master, but he was covering his bases. Both Rhys and I wore wires.

"Let's go." I said. I'd borrowed an ermine coat with roomy pockets and elbow-length white evening gloves from Neldene, but the dress was new. A mere wisp of red beaded silk, and skimpy to boot. Rhys gave me his arm and we crossed the street to where the Dusey was waiting in line.

The double doors to the studio opened for a new arrival, and I caught a glimpse inside. A live jive band was wailing out a tune from the raised bandstand. The dance floor was crowded with dozens of couples, all dressed in the Roaring 20s theme. Opposite the band, on a raised terrace of ornate tables and elegant gilt chairs, I caught a glimpse of Maestro moving smoothly from table to table, chatting up fat cat investors—some human, some, like Maestro and Stella, feeding on the energy in the room.

We hung back, stalling—waiting for the VIP to disembark. At the door, Stella greeted the new arrivals effusively, her fangs flashing. She was poured into a hot pink satin number and wearing a long red wig. She looked like a vampire Jessica Rabbit. Everyone, it seemed, watched the new arrivals expectantly, only to look away, seemingly disappointed. There's a palpable sense of ...something in the air.

Rhys's suddenly hand tightened on mine.

"Ah, I thought I recognized you."

I'd expected the cloudy eyes of a liver-spotted, sallow-faced old man; bloated by greed and debauchery.

Otto Russ was none of those things.

Pale blue eyes and smooth, unlined skin any model would envy, he looked as fresh and rested as if he'd just returned from a week in the Bahamas. At first glance, he gave the impression of a man in the prime of life with prematurely silver hair. But that was a lie. Otto's lifeline was missing. A piece of the puzzle clicked into place. Rhys had been right. Sometime in the last 20 years, Mad Otto had become something other than human. Most likely, that something was like Maestro and Stella, an energy vamp.

I gave him a quizzical look. "Do I know you?" The music inside flared up every time someone opened the door. I hoped Agent Green was getting this. We'd taken the agent down into the caverns beneath Shore Haven and shown him that the bars and seals which had been put in place six months ago had been cleverly breached. The lock on the basement door to the Amble Inn no longer needed a key.

"Otto Russ at your service." Rhys stiffened as Otto lifted my gloved hand to his lips. "Your date's jealousy rolls off him in waves, but I cannot quite put a finger to your emotions, Matilda."

"Try revulsion," I said, as I leaned into Rhys. He gave it right back to me with interest—that feral look I loved gleamed in his eyes and I knew he was back. We were back. As if we'd never really been apart. How could I have ever doubted it? The realization of it almost overwhelmed me.

Inside, the jive band's drummer began a solo that matched the beat in my head, note for note. We'd gotten Otto to confirm his identity, but Rhys and I both wanted more. The first flakes of snow swirled around us.

"I've waited so long to meet you," he said, giving me a ghastly smile. His teeth were unnaturally white.

The music and my man beside me gave me courage. "What do you want from me?"

"It's not what I want from you," he countered. "It's what I want to give to you. A fortune I have. A future, I am building here. For us." He spread his arms magnanimously. "I can offer you immortality. When the time comes, you will not be sorry. For a select few, Shore Haven will be our private hunting ground."

He seemed so sure of himself.

I shuddered. No way. "Immortality? With you? Not in a million years."

His eyes narrowed. "You misunderstand my intentions." He cut a hard glance at Rhys. "You're far too old for my tastes. I prefer my fruit freshly plucked. Unsullied. As you have no progeny, I think Mina--."

The ketamine dart from Rhys's pistol took Otto in the heart, while mine hit Otto below the belt with a satisfying thwap. A third dart, from one of the undercover agents working as a parking valet hit him in the neck.

The feds had Otto out of there in seconds. No one inside had the slightest clue that their guest of honor had just been waylaid. This was a sting, not a raid. The tank of liquid nitrogen was parked a block away, in the parking lot of the Germantown Meat packing plant. Ironically, another of Otto's real estate holdings.

With Otto gone, and his wealth and real estate holdings confiscated, his plans for turning Shore Haven into a flytrap for rich prey would never materialize. The snarl in the fabric of Shore Haven's fate had been smoothed in a way that not even Morta's power could touch.

It was past midnight by the time Green took pity on us and let us leave. The expected storm was upon us and visibility was almost nil by the time Rhys pulled up to the old Queen Anne. He pulled me close and kissed my neck. "You looked so good tonight," he murmured. "It's a shame we didn't get to go dancing."

I laughed. "I'm *never* taking another dance lesson from the Maestro. We're going to have to take them down too, eventually."

"Yep." His eyes never left mine. "But I don't care about that right now." He picked me up and carried me inside like I was nothing. "Come on, beautiful," he said, setting me down. "Dance with me."

I stepped out of the thick fur coat and into his arms. We didn't need music; it was humming in our bones. I melted against the heat of his hard, hungry body. He swept me into the empty dining room, and the room fell away. Dancing with Rhys was like slaking my thirst in a cool mountain stream and basking in front of a hot fire at the same time. After so many weeks apart, the music went on and on until I thought I would die from the pent up want of his touch. For a while, the drums in my head were the sound of two hearts beating as one.

Later, when the candles guttered low on the bedside table, Rhys kissed my open palm. "You've changed. You're stronger. Better." He turned my hand over, as if seeing it for the first time. "The stain is gone."

"And from you as well," I answered. "We're survivors." Was it Charlie's poultices? Master Foo's Qhua Bei practice? Nestled beneath the sheltering arm of my naked lover, it didn't much matter anymore. Love was heavy in the air, and this exact moment was kismet—as if the cosmos smiled down upon us.

Rhys was back and I knew in my very soul that we were connected with an irrevocable bond. Just as I had seen in Lance and Robin's future, our paths grew brighter together. Rhys was Rhys and I was me, as unlikely as it seemed, our fates were connected. And there, snug and warm in the midst of a blizzard, I came to understand that the gift of the Fates had come to me for a reason. The gift doesn't belong to me, I'm just the messenger.

I am the oracle. In the paths between possibility and probability I see the connections.

And like the wheel, there is no beginning or end. There is only the path we choose and the people we touch as we travel.

We are all connected.

END

ABOUT THE AUTHOR

Award-winning author Sharon Joss writes science fiction, fantasy and horror. She is the author of seven novels, including *Aurum*, *Brothers of the Fang*, and the alternate history thriller, *Steam Dogs*. In 2015, she won the Writers of the Future Golden Pen award for speculative fiction with her novella, *Stars That Make Dark Heaven Light*. She lives and writes in Oregon. Find out more about her and her books by going to www.sharonjoss.com

AUTHOR'S NOTE

Thank you for giving this book a read. If you enjoyed it, please tell your friends and consider leaving a review on Amazon or Goodreads, even if it's only a line or two; it would make all the difference and would be very much appreciated. If you'd like a quick note when I have a new release, please sign up for my new release mailing list at:

http://bit.ly/1MhS3lb

Your email will never be shared and you can unsubscribe at any time. I'll send you a free e-book right away and occasionally send out information about contests or opportunities to snag review copies).

Hungry for more?
Here's a sneak peek at the opening chapters of
Brothers of the Fang, a novel in the *Mythica*
series by Sharon Joss

OH BROTHER

JUSTIN OWSLEY STOOD in the open doorway, his eyes
drawn to the cage sitting in the middle of the loft. His heart
pained him as he met the glare of the dark-haired man who
paced silently on the far side of the room. The cage fairly
screamed that the owner was a werewolf, but this guy didn't
have any of the tells. His eyes were brown, not amber, like
Justin's. He appeared fit and well muscled, but lacked the
massive neck and shoulders that made weres in human form
so instantly identifiable. He didn't smell like wolf, either.

He glanced at his trip sheet. "You Mike Bane?" The
guy looked tantalizingly familiar but the name didn't ring
a bell. He proffered his card. "I'm with Brothers of the
Fang Charities. You called for a pickup? Says here you're
donating a leather sofa, dining room table, and some boxes
of cooking utensils."

Bane nodded at the room in general as he padded toward
the kitchen counter. "It all goes. Everything but the cage."
Justin directed Torres and Coop to start with the sofa, while

he began stacking the first three of a pile of neatly taped boxes onto the dolly. Down four flights of stairs and into the donation truck, then back up for another load.

"What do you think," Torres asked, as he threw a padded blanket over the sofa. "Is the cage for his girlfriend?"

"No way. He's a lone wolf. There's no bedroom. No bed." Justin handed the boxes up to Coop on the truck. This stop was the first scheduled pickup of the day.

They started back up the stairs for the next load. "You should say something," Torres said. "That guy is burned out. He's hurtin'."

Justin snorted. "Why me? You've been through it, too. Why do I always have to be the one to say something?"

"Cause you can't help yourself."

Justin felt the warmth of their pheromone-infused humor wash over him. "Shut up."

Two hours later, the loft was nearly empty. Bane stood at the built-in breakfast bar, checking his email, his posture rigid, his eyes glued to the screen. He hadn't said a word to them the whole time. Torres gave Justin an eyebrow jerk in Bane's direction as he and Coop left with the big screen television.

"You've donated some real nice stuff here, Mr. Bane. The guys at the center are going to love that big screen. It looks brand new."

Bane eyed him with a wary look.

Torres was right; the guy was on edge. Justin had seen enough Post Traumatic Stress Disorder and Acquired Lycanthropy Virus Syndrome to recognize a guy in trouble.

Most of the donors to Brothers of the Fang were either military veterans or had ALVS, or both. He looked too young to be a vet, but weres didn't age like humans.

"Glad to hear it. I can't use this stuff anymore." He smiled, but his eyes were hard—cop eyes.

What would a cop be doing with a cage in the middle of his living room? Something clicked in Justin's memory. *Oh shit.* His face had been all over the news for weeks. "Hey, I know you. I mean, I saw your picture." The lurid headlines. "You're that werewolf cop."

Bane froze. "I am not a werewolf." A tic jumped at his right eyelid.

Justin took a step back. "That's right; were-cat. I mean, I heard all about you. You're a hero. You got a bad deal, bro. Busted for eating that drug dealer-." Justin stopped at the hunted expression on Bane's face.

"Are we about done here?"

"Um, yeah. You just have to sign here." Justin handed the clipboard to Bane. "Look pal, I didn't mean to offend you or anything, I was just surprised. You're like some kind of celebrity here in Queens. A lot of the Brothers, and me too, we think you got a raw deal. One less dope dealer in this town ought to be celebrated. I can't believe they fired you."

"I wasn't fired." Bane's dark eyes glowered back at him. "I resigned."

"Yeah, sure." Were those werecat eyes? The guy could pass for human, easy.

"If you'll excuse me, I've still got a couple things left to do."

Justin looked around at the now empty loft, and the brittle appearance of the man standing before him. He had to try. "No, wait. Look, I know it's none of my business and all, but I know what you're thinking. I know you're going through a bad time. Shit, man. You lost control of your beast in a bad situation. But that's no reason to off yourself. It can take years to develop that kind of control. We can help you. That's what Brothers of the Fang is here for. That's our purpose. Trust me brother, suicide is not the cure for ALVS."

Bane shook his head. "I don't have ALVS. And I'm not your brother."

The guy was in denial. "I don't believe you. If it was me that got caught eating the brains of that Hector Clemente guy, I'd be pretty upset too. Sometimes the appetites of the beast can get a little out of control in the beginning."

A ghost of a grin flashed across Bane's face. "It's not what you think. I've got a little place on the lake near Canandaigua. I grew up there. It's already furnished, so this stuff won't fit."

"Ah, the Finger Lakes," Justin said. "That's werewolf country." Between the curfews, restrictions, and lack of open spaces nearby, city living didn't agree with most weres. The job opportunities were a lot tougher in rural areas of the state, but the rules were looser, and the Finger Lakes region had unrestricted hunting privileges for werewolves in the High Tor Wilderness Management Area. Thirty thousand acres of backwoods paradise. You could even join a pack. In the city, everyone was a lone wolf.

Bane shoved the clipboard back at him. "Like I said

before, I'm no werewolf."

Justin bit back his response and reached into his hip pocket for his wallet. He thumbed through the cards inside until he found the one he wanted. "Here. This is a good friend of mine, Dr. Sarah Powers. Everybody down there knows Dr. Sarah. She's good people. She can help you learn to control your beast." He held out the card. "In whatever form it may take."

He hesitated, and Justin sent up a little prayer to the First Wolf. *Take it.*

"Thanks." Bane looked at the card briefly before slipping it into his shirt pocket.

Justin nodded. "Good luck to you then, brother."

"Stop saying that. I didn't ask for any of this. If it weren't for you damn werewolves, I'd still have a job. I'm a shifter, not a were." His voice was low and tight. "I'm *nothing* like you."

The heat rose in Justin's face. "Nobody here but us carnivores, Bane."

THE JOLLEY MAN

THE TINKLE OF the bell announced a fresh customer. Tom Jolley glanced up, but it was old man McNabb. "Hey Gale," Tom greeted him. "How's it going? What can I do for you?"

"The grandson borrowed my crankbait kit for the weekend and lost it overboard."

Tom winced. "Oh jeeze." He noticed the twinkle in McNabb's eyes as he neared the counter. Tom knew from long experience that fishing and his grandson were McNabb's two favorite topics. "You bragging or complaining?"

"Well, mebbe you can't remember what it was like when you were seventeen, but I do. He took that pretty new girlfriend of his out on the lake, ifffin' you know what I mean." McNabb wiggled his bushy white eyebrows for emphasis.

Tom led the way down the aisle to the lures section. "You're lucky he didn't sink more than the tackle box."

"Oh, it was an old box. Not any of my good stuff. But I think he'd appreciate having one of his own. Nothing too fancy, but he's gonna need a couple a them crawdads and a good selection of shad and a nice chartreuse."

An hour later Tom had just finished ringing up McNabb's purchases when Mike finally walked in, looking gaunt. "Hey, Pops," he said, softly. "Wanna buy some nightcrawlers?"

"Nah, I've got the best bait in the state right here." Tom hurried around the counter and grabbed his godson in a bear hug. He fought back tears of emotion as Mike lifted him off the ground, nearly squeezing the breath right out of him.

"Put me down, boy." He gave a quick swipe across his eyes. He couldn't stop smiling.

McNabb, other hand, looked like he was going to come unglued any minute. Coming face-to-face with the 'Were-Cop Cannibal of Queens' wasn't going over too well, even though McNabb had one of the few who'd asked him for the real story. Tom hurriedly made the introductions. "Gale, you remember my godson, don't you? This is Mike Bane."

McNabb hesitated, then jutted his chin and shook the younger man's hand. "A course I do. A course you're taller'n I remember. Tom here has been borin' me silly with the news that yer finally movin' back here from the city. A man can't hardly get a word in edgewise these days. What are your plans?"

Mike ran his hand through his hair. "Ah, nothing, yet. Just a little fishing, I guess." He flashed a grin at Tom. "If you're up to it, old man."

Tom snorted, but his heart wasn't in it. So damn good to see him. "I bag my limit every time I go out, boy." Not really a boy anymore, but the beast and the Fae blood in him kept him looking half his age. He did a quick calculation in his head. God, he must be in his mid-forties by now. He looked so much like Mia. She'd always thought Mikey favored his dad, but damn, the boy had his mother's eyes and cheekbones.

He raised an eyebrow at McNabb, and the old geezer took the hint and made a hasty exit. About time. He wondered if this would be the last time he'd see McNabb in the shop. It didn't matter all that much if it was. Mike was home and that was the important thing. He yelled out for the dog. "Farley, get in here, you mutt. Look who's back."

"He's still here?" Mike's eyes widened in disbelief.

"See for yourself." The tall, shaggy deerhound trotted around the corner and paused, his tail fanning the air, graceful as a question mark.

"Hey boy. Remember me?"

The black dog lowered his head and trotted slowly across the tile floor toward Mike. Tom's heart caught in his throat as Mike kneeled down to rub the dog's crinkled ears. Farley groaned with pleasure.

"He does remember." Mike's voice was tight.

"Stop it, you two. You're going to have me bawling like a baby in a minute. Come on, boy. Let's get you settled in." He locked the front door and led the way toward the back of the tackle shop. "The renters moved out last week, and I had Taffy's niece in to clean yesterday. Dinner's at your place. I stocked your fridge with a stringer of fresh-caught brownies and a six pack. Figured we'd have ourselves a nice fry-up."

"Oh man, I haven't had fresh trout in ages. We got any of those potatoes and onions?"

He held the back door open for Mike and the deerhound. "Wouldn't be a fry up without 'em now, would it? Let's get going, I want to have a beer in my hand as I watch the sunset from your Dad's screen porch."

Farley stood at the passenger door of Mike's truck and gave a soft woof.

Mike opened the battered door of his truck. "Is there enough for the mutt?"

The dog leapt inside without a backward glance. Figured. "Nah, the mutt gets dog food. Fish gives him gas. I got you a fresh forty-pound sack."

"I'm not sure it's a good idea for Farley to stay with me, Pops."

"I've had him long enough. He's your kin, not mine, anyway."

* * *

Later, after dinner, they sat out on the screen porch at the back of the house, drinking beer and watching the light fade from the sky. The sailor's delight of a sunset over the lake had been spectacular; like a welcome home banner. They'd both eaten too much and laughed too much, but it was good. Good for both of them. Like a snagged line, suddenly freed, Tom felt they were back on an even keel again.

"This is nice. Most nights it's just me and Farley, and Farley doesn't talk much." He wanted to ask more about the fiasco in Queens, but Mike had always been so secretive about the jaguar. Of course, the press had gotten it wrong, but he couldn't bring himself to break the mood by asking.

They watched the deerhound twitch in his sleep, woofing in that weird way that dogs do when they're dreaming. No doubt chasing rabbits out on the Tor.

"I don't want to hurt him, Pops. He can't stay here. I don't think you understand--"

Tom could feel his godson's growing anxiety itch like sand under his shirt. "Oh I know what you mean. Cats and dogs and all that." Tom slapped at a mosquito. "It'll work or it won't. This isn't the city, boy. This property sits right on the Tor boundary and there's plenty of open space for the both of you. As long as you remember the rules, your beast and the mutt will figure it out."

Mike's face tightened. "The cat stays in the cage at night. I can't take the chance of him hurting anybody." He shook his head. "Ever again."

The haunted look on the boy's face said it all. *He's a grown man*, Tom reminded himself. "Quit worrying about Farley. He can take care of himself. There's plenty of Fae creatures and wild game out there on the Tor. As long as you remain in beast form, it's the perfect place to let the cat out to hunt. All the local weres hunt there, even the Mythica pack. Just remember that the High Tor Fae won't tolerate trespassers in human form. It's beasts only." Tom gave a glance to the dog. "No exceptions."

Mike rubbed at a stain on the arm of the faded blue sofa. "I'm never going out on the Tor again."

"Don't be stupid, boy. You keep that beast of yours caged up too long he'll drive you mad. Just like what happened up there in Queens. Isn't that why you came running back here after all these years?" *Easy*. He's going to have to come to terms with this thing in his own way.

His godson's locked jaw twitched as he stared out across the dusky lake. Whatever happened to that eager, clever lad who was never afraid of anything; who was just brimming with enthusiasm for life? He'd wanted to see the world. Couldn't wait to leave this place. Well, the world pretty much chewed him up and spit him out. Now he's lost his job and his citizenship. He's all alone, living in a cage. *I'd give anything to take that monkey off his back, but I just don't know what to say to him.*

Tom sighed. Maybe Farley would help. Couldn't hurt. Taking care of the dog would give Mike something to do, at least. Even if the dog didn't need it.

"I could use a hand at the store," he lied.

"No you don't. I saw the look on McNabb's face. It took real guts for him to shake my hand. I'm sure everybody in town knows about me by now. Or thinks they do."

"You know how fast gossip spreads around here. We've grown a bit, but Canandaigua is still the same small town it used to be." And that was the bitch of it. It didn't matter that Mike was a local boy, or that he wasn't infected with ALVS, or that he didn't even look like a lycan. They'd tarred him with the same brush anyway. "We're a tourist town; lycans are bad for business. Finding a job here might be difficult."

Mike gave him a tight-lipped smile. "Thanks for the offer. I just don't think I'm cut out for waiting on customers all day. You're the one they come in to talk to. Having me around is bound to affect your business. Maybe coming here wasn't such a good idea."

"Don't say that." Tom couldn't stand the thought. "I don't care what McNabb or any of them think. You'll never see a 'No Lycans Served' sign in the window of my shop. As far as I'm concerned, lycan money is as good as anyone's, and I'm not the only one around here that thinks that way. You should stop in at Taffy's place. He'll be glad to help you out with a job."

"Take it easy, Pops." Mike put a calming hand on his arm. "I don't need a job just yet. I need a little time to figure things out, that's all."

Tom pressed his lips into a firm line. *The last thing that boy needs is time on his hands to brood.* A sudden inspiration struck him. "Hey, I got it. I had McNabb's grandson all lined up to make my bait deliveries for the summer, but he's met some girl up near Syracuse and backed out at the last minute. It's been a real pain for me. Would you do it?"

The boyish grin he remembered flashed across Mike's face.

"It's only three days a week. You'll be done by mid-morning, latest. You already know most of the route. It'll be like old times. Say yes. Make an old man happy."

"Don't give me that old man shit. You've barely aged a day since I've been gone. You've got almost as much Fae blood in you as I do."

"Come on. I've got nobody else and you've got plenty of time on your hands."

"Sure Pops; no problem." Mike popped him playfully in the shoulder.

"Good. It's settled then."

Farley heaved a contented sigh and farted.

THE HAPPY HUNTER

MIKE STALKED THE rooms of the cottage while Farley snored soundly in the middle of the king-sized bed in the larger of the two bedrooms. The house was much as he remembered, although he hadn't been back since he'd become a shifter. He'd set up the cage in the smaller bedroom--empty except for a beat-up wooden desk and chair. Thick shrubbery covered most of the front of the house, shielding it from the frontage road and keeping the room preternaturally dark.

The cage was six by six foot square and four feet high. It was actually a lion cage made with a stainless steel knotted wire rope mesh; the same mesh used for animal enclosures by zoos. He'd had the cage custom made of six panels that he could assemble with a socket wrench in about twenty minutes. A simple mechanism kept the cat safely contained; a human thumb was required to open the door. The enclosure was a hated reminder of his condition; but he'd been sleeping in the cage nearly half his life.

Mike could feel the cat's restlessness inside him. If the cat wasn't allowed to roam free for a few hours every four or five days, the tenuous truce between them started to fall apart. Tom had urged him to let the cat do a little investigation of the territory, and maybe he was right. It wouldn't hurt to let the cat out before he locked himself inside the cage for the night. In the city, the closest wilderness area took at least two hours to get to. He'd drive to Moose River or the Adirondacks whenever he could, but working undercover made it difficult to keep to a schedule that kept the cat happy. And keeping the cat happy was paramount.

He checked to make sure the back yard gate was locked; not that it mattered. The closest house was a quarter mile up the road. No six-foot fence would hold him, and the cat was an excellent swimmer. He loved the water, and the property had its own private dock.

Seated on the faded blue divan on the sun porch, where they'd hoisted beers and filled their bellies earlier, Mike stripped out of his clothes and folded them neatly beside him. He took a deep breath, closed his eyes, and let go.

The melting sensation flowed through him, familiar and soothing now, after all those wasted years he'd spent fighting it. Instead of the bone-breaking agony the werewolves had to endure, his cat came forth like the unfurling of a flag. Only the final sensation of fur emerging through his skin tickled, but a good shake always put him right. That was one of the few blessings that came with being a shape-shifter rather than a werewolf.

All lycanthropes were shape-shifters, but not all shape-shifters were lycanthropes. Acquired Lycanthropy Virus Syndrome was a disease that altered the genetics of the afflicted. People with ALVS lost control over their ability to maintain their inherent species form, particularly during stressful conditions such as rage or the three nights of the full moon.

In spite of the brutality of the manner in which he'd acquired his shifting abilities, Mike appreciated that he had no such tie with the cycles of the moon, and felt no physical discomfort with the change. The Nagual had come to him as two separate spirits. The jaguar was one of them. Unlike the weres, the big cat's body, mind and thoughts were separate from his own.

The cat stretched fully, and trotted out the door to one of the big pines in the back yard. With his front paws, he reached as high as he could stretch and dug his claws into the rough bark. Clots of bark and dried pitch flew out from the trunk as he drew his claws deep into the tree and scratched deep grooves into the wood. The gouge pattern mirrored the landscape of the Finger Lakes the region; the long narrow glacial lakes that that local legends said were made by the claws of the Great Bear spirit of the Senequois Fae clan.

The sharp tang of fresh evergreen stung the air, dulling the scent of fresh blood and fish scraps wafting out from the garbage can. The jaguar dropped to the ground and rolled in the grass, exorcising the pent-up stress of the day. The cat liked this place, he could tell.

Seeing the world through his beast's eyes never failed to thrill him. Unlike the weres, he retained complete memory of every moment spent in jaguar form. He didn't control the big guy's actions or thinking; it was more like riding shotgun in some armored ATV in the jungle whenever the cat went hunting. He could make general suggestions, but the cat was always in control.

The jaguar's night vision was every bit as good as human vision, although the cat's sense of color was more subdued. When the cat was in charge, his color spectrum was limited to greens, blues, purples, and greys. The cat was uncomfortable in open spaces, and would avoid them whenever possible. The concept of terrain was physical texture that only mattered where it touched him. He rubbed against rough pillars of tree trunks and slunk his way through cheek-high grasses as he sought dense shrubs for hiding under.

The cat's ability to track and scent prey never failed to amaze him, and for such a big animal, he made very little noise. The cat was careful and cautious in the new environment, but there was nothing for him to fear.

The big guy was an ambush hunter. He preferred to wait for his prey to come to him, although he'd surprised and successfully brought down deer and even a bear once. His favored prey was rabbits, turkey, opossums, and if he could find them, turtles, but he wasn't really picky. If he didn't make a kill, he went hungry, but that was a rare occurrence. After all the fish Mike had eaten at dinner, the cat wouldn't be interested in hunting tonight.

After a quick dip in the lake, the cat settled beneath a dogwood tree and began to groom himself. Mike could feel the jaguar's deep satisfaction and contentment in a way that he'd never experienced before. With the bats calling overhead as they plucked mosquitoes out of the night sky, the enchantment of the lake settled over them.

If only it could stay like this. He'd forgotten how peaceful life was on the lake. *If only it was just the cat and me. We could live a pretty good life like this. Things would be different this time.* Maybe Tehuantl would succumb to the magic of this place and settle down, too. If he could keep the cat content, there would be no way for the psychotic shaman spirit to manifest. Tehuantl, sacred priest of the ancient Jaguar-people of Central America, was unstoppable once he came out. When Tehuantl came out, people died.

Mike shivered at a phantom memory of the taste of Hector Clemente's brains. He'd been damn lucky it was a drug dealer and not somebody's mother, he thought. *I was kidding myself, thinking I could keep it a secret.* But it was too late now; everyone assumed he had ALVS.

The landmark case of Stubbs versus the State of

Tennessee had changed everything. William Stubbs, a US Army veteran, had sued the state of Tennessee for wrongful termination when he was laid off from his job for excessive sick days. He'd claimed the State had discriminated against him due to his ALVS by counting his moon-days as sick days. The State counter-sued, claiming that lycanthropes weren't human, and therefore not entitled to the same benefits. They pointed to the definition of 'man' in the US Constitution, the differences in DNA, the unique blood type, and the fact that transplant organs from lycanthropes were always rejected when used on humans. The State of Tennessee won, and the US Supreme Court upheld the appeal. Four short years later, the 28th amendment redefined the term 'man' to exclude homo lycanthropus.

Lycans had had their citizenship downgraded to permanent resident status. They'd had their passports revoked, lost the right to vote, put on the no-fly list, and had to have a green card in order to get a job. They had a curfew. Discrimination was rampant; not even contact lenses could hide a 28-inch neck. Mike had been on the force when the amendment passed, and decided to keep his status as a shape-shifter to himself. Even so, the guy from Brothers of the Fang hadn't believed him when he'd told him he wasn't a werewolf. He'd hoped to lay low here for a while until things blew over. Until Tom confirmed it, he hadn't really believed the area had become such a haven for werewolves.

So be it. At least I've come to the right place. No more living undercover.

Tom was right. He'd kept the cat caged far too much.

Besides, if there were that many wolves running loose down here, why shouldn't the cat be allowed the same privilege?

As long as the cat was happy, it was the two of them against Tehuantl, and that was all that really mattered. And that meant letting the jaguar out on a regular basis.

The sound of a lone wolf howl echoed across the Tor. The cat paused his grooming to listen, but it was not repeated.

I'm not like them. They can't control themselves, they're animals. I don't have a disease. I'm still human, or at least partly. Clemente had been an aberration; the disastrous result of extraordinary circumstances. *If I'd shot him, they'd have given me a medal and I'd still be a damn good cop.*

The cat yawned and stretched, then sauntered toward the house. It paused in the sun porch, and Mike mentally nudged at the cat to release him, but the feline resisted, moseying instead past the cage toward the back bedroom. It stopped in the doorway to the master bedroom as Farley whimpered in sleep in the middle of the bed. The cat's ears pricked forward at the sound.

Too late, Mike realized that this could end very badly. He pushed harder against the cat. The cat knew the drill here; it was just being stubborn. *Into the cage, pal.*

In a single leap, the jaguar cleared the distance and landed on the bed next to the curled-up canine. The deerhound cracked an eye, but didn't move. Carefully, the cat settled up against the warm dog and a rumbled purr arose from the deep inside his chest.

Relief flooded through Mike. *Well what do you know. He likes dogs.*

BROTHERS OF THE FANG

by Sharon Joss

is available from all your favorite book and e-book retailers